ORDINARY LIVES, EXTRAORDINARY STORIES

SHORT STORIES BY AJAY DUSANE

ISBN
Paperback 979-8-89544-895-3
Hardcase 979-8-89588-375-4

Dedication

I dedicate this book to my *Father*,
who was my guiding light and source of inspiration,
and to my *Mother*,
whose tireless efforts to educate us shaped me
into the person I am today.

About the Book

This book is more than just a collection of short stories; it represents a journey—a journey that has spanned over years, from the first spark of inspiration to the final words on the page. It is a sum of the curiosity I have about the human mind. It's my debut as an author, and while the act of writing came easily once I began, the process of bringing these stories to life required patience, reflection, and a deep connection to the world around me. Years of travel, deeply observing people, and a will to make a difference have helped me put the stories together.

The stories within these pages are the result of years of observing people – their behaviours, their interactions, and the subtle ways they navigate through life. Each character, each scenario, is a reflection of the human experience as I have come to understand it. They are stories that were brewing in my mind long before they found their way to paper, and I'm delighted to finally share them with you.

Growing up in Pune, a city that has been a constant companion throughout my life, has had a profound influence on me. Pune is a city of contrasts—where the old meets the new, where bustling streets give way to quiet corners, and where tradition blends seamlessly with modernity. I've walked its streets, explored its hidden alleys, and absorbed its essence. This city, with all its charm and character, is the backdrop to many of my stories. But while the settings may be distinctly Pune, the themes they explore are universal.

The stories in this book delve into the intricacies of human nature, capturing the emotions, struggles, and triumphs that define our existence. They remind us of the importance of the small moments—those fleeting instances of joy, connection, and introspection that often get lost in the rush of everyday life. In these stories, you'll find a celebration of relationships, a reflection on the challenges we face, and a deep appreciation for the journey of life itself.

Though I come from a professional background in marketing, this book is not a product of that world. It's a deeply personal endeavour, born from my own experiences, emotions, and observations. It's written from the perspective of someone who has always been fascinated by the human mind and who believes in the power of stories to connect us all. This book is not about selling an idea; it's about sharing a piece of my soul.

I hope that as you read these stories, you'll find something that resonates with you – whether it's a lesson, a memory, or simply a feeling that stays with you long after you've turned the last page. And perhaps, you'll feel inspired to share these stories with others, passing along the emotions and insights that you've discovered within these pages.

Ajay Dusane

Contents

Contents

Chapter 1

Tribal Affair

The tin roof of the outhouse was making a rhythmic sound, a steady drumbeat of raindrops that echoed through the air. Sanjay could hear the rains pouring down, a symphony of nature's percussion. He loved the rainy season, especially in the Satupuda's, where the monsoons transformed the landscape into a lush, vibrant green. The earthy scent of petrichor filled the air, mingling with the fresh, cool breeze that swept through the quarters.

As he sat in the old government quarter, a relic of a bygone era, with a cup of steaming tea in his hands, the warm, comforting aroma of the tea mingled with the scent of rain. He watched the raindrops as they cascaded down the leaves, each drop glistening like a tiny crystal before merging into a larger stream that trickled off the edges. The window panes were dotted with droplets, each one creating a small ripple as it joined its companions in a watery dance.

These were the moments Sanjay cherished, moments of solitude where he could let his thoughts wander freely. The rhythmic sound of the rain was a soothing backdrop as he delved into his memories and creative musings. His mind often wandered to the "what ifs" of life, the paths not taken, and the possibilities that lay ahead. The rain seemed to wash away the present, leaving him with a blank canvas to paint his thoughts and dreams.

In these quiet times, the rain was more than just a weather phenomenon; it was a muse, a companion, and a trigger for introspection. The steady downpour outside mirrored the flow of his thoughts, a constant, calming presence that allowed him to explore the depths of his imagination.

Sanjay, at 17, was a young man on the cusp of adulthood, brimming with a unique blend of curiosity and introspection. He stood tall with a lean build, his frame suggesting the promise of strength yet to come. His hair was a tousled mop of dark waves, often falling into his intense, thoughtful eyes. Those eyes, a deep shade of brown, were windows to his inquisitive mind, always reflecting a sense of wonder and contemplation.

He was an avid reader, often found with a book in his hands, losing himself in worlds far removed from his own. His favourite genres were fantasy and historical fiction, as they allowed him to escape and explore different eras and realms. This love for reading had cultivated in him a rich imagination and a talent for storytelling. Sanjay often would pen down his thoughts and stories in a worn-out notebook he carried everywhere, filling its pages with his dreams and reflections.

Academically, Sanjay was diligent and curious, excelling in subjects that challenged his intellect, particularly science and literature. He had a keen interest in how things work, often taking apart gadgets at home to understand their mechanics. Despite his academic prowess, he remains humble, always eager to learn from others and share his knowledge with others.

Socially, Sanjay was reserved, preferring the company of a few close friends over large groups. He was a good listener, always lending a sympathetic ear and offering thoughtful advice. His friends would appreciate his calm demeanour and the way he could see things from different perspectives.

Sanjay had a deep appreciation for nature, particularly the monsoon season. He found solace in the rhythm of the rain, the scent of wet earth, and the sight of lush greenery. These natural elements often inspired his creative thoughts and provided a backdrop for his introspective moments.

In terms of family, Sanjay shared a close bond with his parents and younger sister. He respected his parents deeply and valued their guidance, though he was beginning to carve out his own path and opinions. His sister looked up to him, and he always took his role as an elder sibling seriously, always looking out for her and offering support.

Sanjay's father was an officer at the State Bank of India branch, posted in a small village near the Maharashtra-Gujarat border. The family lived in modest government quarters, a place marked by its simplicity and the close-knit community it fostered. These quarters, while not luxurious, were filled with warmth and the subtle charm of a small-town life.

Every morning, Sanjay's father donned his crisp, white shirt and neatly pressed trousers, a testament to his disciplined nature and pride in his work. With a sense of purpose, he would walk to the nearby bank branch, a short distance that allowed him to greet neighbours and exchange pleasantries with shopkeepers and locals along the way. His presence in the town was well-known and respected, a reliable figure in the community.

Sanjay admired his father's dedication and work ethic, seeing in him a model of responsibility and integrity. His father's daily walks to the bank were more than a routine; they symbolised a steady commitment to his role and the community he served. This environment, grounded in the values of hard work and simplicity, shaped Sanjay's own outlook on life.

Sanjay's mother, a homemaker, kept the household running smoothly, her days filled with chores and the occasional visit from neighbours. The family lived a simple yet fulfilling life, with routines that brought a comforting rhythm to their days. Meals were shared together, often filled with laughter, discussions about the day's events, and dreams for the future.

The quarters themselves, though basic, were surrounded by greenery, with a small garden that Sanjay's mother tended to with care. The sound of birds chirping in the morning and the rustle of leaves in the evening were constant companions. The monsoon season would transform this little garden into a lush, vibrant space, a favourite spot for Sanjay to retreat with his books and thoughts.

The small town, with its narrow streets and familiar faces, was a place where everyone knew each other and life moved at a gentle, unhurried pace. The proximity to both Maharashtra and Gujarat brought a blend of cultures, enriching the community with diverse traditions and festivals. This multicultural atmosphere played a role in broadening Sanjay's understanding of the world, fostering a sense of inclusiveness and curiosity about different ways of life.

Sanjay's time in this setting, amidst the monsoon rains and the daily rhythm of small-town life, instilled in him a deep appreciation for the simple joys and a reflective mindset. It was a nurturing environment that allowed his imagination to flourish, his thoughts to deepen, and his character to be shaped by the values of his family and community.

When Sanjay usually returned from his studies in Pune, where he stayed with his aunt, the quarters offered him a welcome retreat. Every 2-3 months, during his short visits, he would soak in the tranquillity of the place. The silence of the quarters, punctuated only by the soft whoosh of the wind and the gentle rustling of leaves, created a serene backdrop for his reflections.

The variety of bird species in the area, each with its own unique chirping pattern and distinctive colours, added to the peaceful ambiance. Sanjay found comfort in their melodies, which seemed to echo his own inner musings. He would often take long walks around the trees, immersing himself in the natural beauty that surrounded him. Each rustle of leaves and chirp of a bird felt amplified, drawing him deeper into his thoughts.

These moments of solitude allowed Sanjay to disconnect from the demands of his academic life and reconnect with his own sense of purpose. The serenity of the quarters, combined with the ever-present reminder of nature's rhythms, provided a perfect setting for contemplating his life and what lay ahead.

The days in the quarters moved at a gentle, deliberate pace, a stark contrast to the fast-paced rhythm of city life. Unlike the frenetic energy of the metro where people seemed to rush past, often missing the simple joys of stillness, the small-town life offered a slower, more reflective tempo.

Sanjay would rise early, around six, without the need for an alarm. The natural sounds of the morning—the gentle chirping of birds and the soft rustling of leaves—served as his wake-up call. Light would seep through the tall windows, casting a warm glow that signalled the start of a new day.

Mornings in the quarters were a flurry of activity. His mother, already up and ready, would be engaged in her daily rituals, finishing her round of pooja with quiet devotion. By the time she made the tea, she was also preparing to start on her new design for the rangoli, a colourful pattern she would create on the floor. Meanwhile, his father completed his own round of pooja, adding to the rhythmic harmony of the morning.

The maid, a local Adivasi (tribal) woman, arrived early each day. Her presence was a familiar part of the routine, and the sound of her washing utensils punctuated the quiet of the early morning. Dishwashers and washing machines were still a distant luxury at that time, so the maids handled all the household chores. They were considered as integral to the household as any family member, sharing meals and participating in the daily life of the family. Though they spoke only broken Marathi, their efforts and presence bridged the gap, allowing them to be part of the cultural fabric of the home.

These moments of early morning calm, combined with the simplicity and communal spirit of the quarters, provided Sanjay with a profound sense of connection and peace. It was a time for him to appreciate the stillness, the warmth of family routines, and the rhythm of life that contrasted sharply with the bustling world outside.

Sanjay's morning routine was a comforting ritual. An early bath to refresh himself, followed by a quiet pooja to start the day with mindfulness, and then a hot breakfast paired with a steaming cup of tea. It was a serene way to begin his day, setting a positive tone before the world outside began to stir.

By 9:00 AM, his father would head off to the bank branch, leaving Sanjay and his mother to continue their day. His mother, with her love for literature, would immerse herself in her novels, losing herself in their pages. Sanjay, having developed a fondness for reading her books since the age of 12, shared this literary passion. Her novels had captivated him, and he found himself drawn into the worlds they depicted.

As he sat in the quiet of the quarters, perhaps gazing out into the lush greenery or lost in thought, Sanjay would often reflect on the stories he had read. His imagination, sparked by these novels, began to envision his own narratives, planting the seeds for his future writing aspirations. He would daydream about crafting his own stories, aspiring to one day create a novel of his own, blending his experiences and creativity into a unique literary work.

These moments of solitude, surrounded by the calming routine and the influence of his mother's novels, nurtured his creativity and ambition, giving him a sense of purpose and a glimpse into the possibilities of his future as a writer.

The afternoons were accompanied by the comforting aroma of his mother's cooking, filling the quarters with a sense of home. His mother's love for cooking was evident in every detail—her meticulous planning, organising, and the care she put into each meal. When Sanjay was around, she would prepare her best dishes, often adding a special treat of sweets to make the meal even more enjoyable.

The rhythm of village life, with its natural pace and serene environment, made the afternoon siesta a delightful necessity. The absence of air conditioners was never a concern. The weather, influenced by the monsoon and winter seasons, was always pleasantly cool.

Evenings in the quarters were lively with the presence of father's office colleagues and spouses, family friends, and neighbours at times. These visits brought a flurry of chatter and laughter, adding a social vibrancy to the tranquil setting. Sanjay would often sit quietly, nodding along, smiling, or simply observing the interactions. The conversations were accompanied by the familiar routine of serving tea, sometimes refilling cups, and enjoying the shared warmth of these moments.

In the background, the soothing presence of *'All India Radio'* added another layer to the evening atmosphere. Programmes like Jaymala, Bhule Bisre Geet, and Cibaca Geet Mala filled the air with music from bygone eras. The occasional cricket commentary and news updates also found their way into the conversation, blending seamlessly with the social buzz.

The music of those years left a lasting impression on Sanjay. The melodies and lyrics became intertwined with his memories of the house, creating a nostalgic soundtrack for his youth. Whenever he heard those songs again, they had the magical ability to transport him back to those evenings, evoking the sights, sounds, and feelings of home. The music was not just a backdrop but a key part of the sensory experience that defined his cherished memories of family gatherings and simple joys.

The rains had taken a brief respite, and the sun, shedding its earlier reticence, peered through the clouds, casting a gentle warmth over the morning. It was a pleasant day, with a renewed vibrancy in the air. Even the birds, sensing the shift in weather, had emerged from their nests, their cheerful songs mingling with the gentle breeze.

Sanjay, savouring his cup of tea, pulled his chair closer to the window. As he sipped, he gazed out at the garden, enjoying the serene beauty of the freshly washed landscape. The rain had left a clean, invigorating scent in the air, and the garden seemed to sparkle with renewed life.

He noticed a tribal girl in the garden, her movements graceful and deliberate as she bent to gather flowers that had fallen to the ground. The flowers, white and delicate, seemed to have been scattered like a soft, natural carpet beneath the tree. The tribal girl carefully collected these blooms, her head cover fashioned into a loop which she used to gather and transport the carefully picked flowers.

Sanjay watched with quiet admiration as she worked. The simplicity of her task, combined with the artistry of nature's display, created a peaceful scene. The girl's attention to detail and the care with which she handled the flowers reflected a deep connection to her surroundings.

The tribal girl wore a striking black blouse paired with a plain pink sari, which was characteristic of the attire in this region. The tribal dress style here was distinct, often showcasing a blend of practicality and cultural expression. The blouse, though simple, accentuated the contours of the wearer, while the cotton sari, typically a single colour, was wrapped neatly around her body. It was secured with one end draped over her head, offering both utility and modesty.

The tribal clothing was often complemented by silver jewellery, adding a touch of elegance to their traditional attire. She wore chains around her neck, adorned with coins—often large, such as a 10-rupee coin—along with an arm band and a vest chain that ran across her navel. These pieces of jewellery were not just decorative, but also carried cultural significance.

One notable aspect of tribal women's appearance in this region was their tattoos. These were small, intricately designed, and often placed where women would traditionally wear their Bindi. The tattoos were artful, minimalistic, and seemed to reflect the wearer's personality and connection to nature. Many tribal women also had their names tattooed on their forearms, adding a personal touch to their body art.

The tribals typically lived in the jungles or mountainous regions, and walking was their primary mode of transport. This lifestyle contributed to their robust physical fitness, with older individuals often maintaining a strong and agile physique. Tribal women, in particular, were known for their well-toned, curvaceous figures, a testament to their active lifestyle and the natural harmony of their environment.

As Sanjay sat by the window, sipping his tea and watching the girl in the garden, he could only glimpse her from a distance. The window frame obscured her face, but he noticed details that intrigued him. She was taller than most; her legs were toned and strong, and she seemed to be more robust than the others. Her long fingers worked delicately as she gathered the flowers, and her well-defined figure moved with a certain grace.

Driven by curiosity, Sanjay set down his cup of tea and walked out to the veranda, eager to get a closer look. He hoped to see her face, to understand the person behind the graceful movements and the meticulous care she took in collecting the fallen flowers.

As he approached, the tribal girl became aware of his presence. With surprising speed, she gathered her flowers. Her movements were sharp and purposeful as she darted away from the garden.

Sanjay's heart sank as he watched her run off, disappearing into the distance. He stood on the veranda, feeling a pang of disappointment that he had been unable to see her face. The fleeting encounter left him with more questions than answers. Why had she fled so suddenly? Was there something about his presence that had startled her, or was it simply that she preferred to keep her anonymity?

The mystery of the tribal girl lingered in his mind, her sudden departure adding an air of intrigue to the serene morning. Sanjay found himself wondering if he would ever have another chance to see her, to uncover the story behind her fleeting appearance, and to discover the face that had so captivated his curiosity.

The tribal girl occupied Sanjay's thoughts throughout the day, her image becoming a vivid mental sketch that he couldn't shake. Every moment seemed to revolve around her, as he tried to piece together what her face might look like and what kind of person she might be. Her brief appearance had touched something deep within him, stirring emotions he couldn't quite define.

For the first time, Sanjay experienced a blend of anxiety, happiness, and exhilaration all at once. The feeling was unfamiliar and intense, leaving him restless and intrigued. His mind replayed the scene over and over, trying to fill in the gaps left by her sudden departure.

As the evening descended, Sanjay found himself listening to the familiar songs on All India Radio, their melodies weaving through the quiet of the quarters. The music, once a backdrop to his days, now seemed to resonate with his heightened emotions. Each song stirred his heart, amplifying his feelings and adding layers of nostalgia and longing.

The combination of the music and his thoughts about the tribal girl created a rich tapestry of emotions. He felt a profound connection to the melodies that seemed to echo his inner turmoil. The songs became a soundtrack to his yearning and curiosity, capturing the essence of the stirring emotions that had taken hold of him.

Sanjay's day was consumed by the enigma of the tribal girl, leaving him in a state of reflective restlessness. The fleeting encounter had sparked a deeper introspection, and as he listened to the evening's broadcast, he found himself lost in a blend of longing and wonder, eager to uncover more about the mysterious girl who had so unexpectedly captured his imagination.

Barely able to sleep through the night, Sanjay woke up earlier than usual the next morning, his mind already preoccupied with thoughts of the tribal girl. He was unsure if he would see her again, but hoped for another glimpse. As he sipped his cup of tea, he sat by the window, his gaze fixed outside with hopeful anticipation.

His heart skipped a beat when he finally spotted her in the garden. Her back was turned towards him, but Sanjay noticed the flowers she had collected the previous day were now elegantly tucked into her hair. She was busy gathering more flowers, moving with the same grace and skill that had captivated him before.

Determined not to miss any detail, Sanjay remained in his chair, hoping for a better view. Despite his efforts to adjust his position and catch a glimpse of her face, she remained elusive, always keeping her back towards him. It felt as though she was aware of his presence and deliberately teasing him, a silent game that she seemed to be winning effortlessly.

Today, she wore a fresh red sari, which contrasted with the more muted pink from the previous day. The vibrant colour added to her allure, making her presence even more striking. Sanjay noticed the new sari; its brightness was a stark reminder of her deliberate attempts to remain out of view.

In his frustration and curiosity, Sanjay moved to another window, hoping to find a new angle. Yet, as he shifted, she turned away, furthering the sense of playful avoidance. It was as if they were engaged in an unspoken game, with her successfully evading his gaze at every turn.

Feeling a mix of excitement and exasperation, Sanjay decided to run out to the veranda, hoping to catch a final glimpse before she disappeared. But, by the time he reached the garden, she had already gone, leaving him with a sense of defeat and unfulfilled curiosity.

Her departure left Sanjay with heightened emotions and a deep sense of intrigue. The morning's encounter had intensified his feelings, and the game she seemed to play had only fuelled his desire to know more. As he stood alone on the veranda, he couldn't help but feel that their brief, elusive interactions had woven a complex web of curiosity and longing, making him all the more eager to see her again.

Sanjay spent the entire day in a sombre mood, weighed down by the thought of his impending departure for Pune. The realisation that he had only a week left in the quarters filled him with a sense of melancholy. He couldn't quite pinpoint the emotions stirring within him—whether it was excitement, happiness, or something else entirely. This internal confusion only deepened his sense of unease.

As the evening arrived, Sanjay turned on the radio, seeking solace in the romantic songs that played softly. The melodies, once a pleasant backdrop, now seemed to resonate with a deeper significance. The lyrics spoke to him in a way they hadn't before, and he found himself reflecting on their meanings with a newfound intensity.

The romantic tunes stirred feelings of remorse and loneliness, as if his heart had skipped a beat. The music captured the essence of what he was experiencing, an emotional turbulence that mingled with the sense of impending loss.

His mind wandered back to the garden where the tribal girl had stood, her carved figure etched into his memory as she faced away from him. The image of her, so close yet so distant, seemed to embody the complex emotions he was grappling with. The fleeting encounter, her elusive presence, and the mystery surrounding her had left an indelible mark on him.

That night, Sanjay resolved to confront the elusive flower girl, no matter what came his way. Determined to seize the chance before he left, he woke up earlier than usual the next morning. After his morning tea, he ventured into the garden, strolling and waiting with a mix of anticipation and resolve.

As he walked, his heart raced with both hope and trepidation. He turned back to check if she had arrived, and in an instant, his heart skipped a beat. There, she was standing twenty metres away, her presence both breathtaking and surreal.

She was dressed in a purple sari and a white blouse, her outfit adding a striking contrast to the previous days. Her hair was tied back, with curls falling delicately on either side of her forehead. The rich, deep brown of her eyes matched the colour of her hair, and her thin lips curved into a smile that seemed capable of breaking through any barrier. Her eyes held a magnetic allure, capable of piercing through hearts and stirring emotions.

Sanjay felt as if the ground had been pulled from beneath him. The shock and awe of seeing her so clearly left him momentarily disoriented. He stood rooted to the spot, unable to move, as their gazes locked. The world around them seemed to fade away, leaving just the two of them in a silent, intimate exchange.

For what felt like ten minutes, they stared at each other, their eyes speaking volumes without uttering a single word. It was as if their hearts were conversing in a language beyond words, bridging the gap between them with unspoken understanding and connection. The silence between them was charged with a deep, emotional resonance, each of them attempting to convey feelings and thoughts that words could not capture.

In that fleeting moment, Sanjay experienced a profound sense of connection, as if their souls had touched and communicated in the silence. The encounter, brief yet intense, left him with an overwhelming sense of awe and a feeling that something significant had passed between them.

Sanjay was overwhelmed by a profound realisation. He had fallen deeply in love for the first time. The tribal girl's beauty had instantly captivated him, and he found himself mesmerised by her every move. Her elegance, her curvy figure, and the way she carried herself had stirred emotions within him that were entirely new.

As she continued to pick her flowers with the same grace, Sanjay's gaze was drawn to her, unable to tear away from her form. The way she moved, the soft curve of her body, and her radiant smile had an almost hypnotic effect on him. He felt a surge of passion and admiration unlike anything he had experienced before. Her beauty and the silent exchange they shared had etched a lasting impression on his heart.

When she looked back one last time and smiled before leaving, Sanjay's heart ached with longing. He watched her graceful figure recede into the distance, realising that she had carved a special place in his heart. At that moment, he knew that this girl would forever hold a cherished spot in his memory.

The following days were consumed by thoughts of her. Sanjay found himself daydreaming about their future together, imagining a life where they could be together. He was acutely aware of the stark differences between their lives and the unlikely chance that their paths would ever truly intersect. Yet, his feelings were so strong that he couldn't help but hope for a future that seemed almost impossible.

With only a few days left before his departure, Sanjay was determined to make the most of his remaining time. He planned to speak to her, to confess his feelings, hold her hand, and kiss her. The intensity of his emotions led to restless nights as he was unable to sleep, his mind consumed by visions of her and the life they might share. His heart raced with anticipation and uncertainty, caught in the bittersweet reality of his fleeting yet profound connection with the tribal girl.

With his departure for Pune imminent, Sanjay was filled with a mix of sadness and urgency. His bus to the district town was scheduled for 12 o'clock in the afternoon the next day, and he knew that time was running out. As he pondered over what to say to the flower girl, he felt a deep sense of melancholy about leaving.

The final night before his departure was excruciating for Sanjay. He tossed and turned, unable to find rest, his mind racing with thoughts of the tribal girl. Each glance at the clock seemed to heighten his anxiety, and he was acutely aware that only a few precious hours remained before he had to leave.

As dawn approached, he lay in bed, his heart set on expressing his feelings to her as soon as she appeared to pick the flowers. The thought of finally confessing his love filled him with a mixture of nervous excitement and longing.

Suddenly, his mother's voice cut through his restless state. "Sanjay, Sanjay," she called, attempting to wake him. Bleary-eyed, Sanjay glanced at the clock and realised with a jolt that it was already 9:00 AM. Panic surged through him as he leaped out of bed, his mind racing. He had fallen into a deep sleep and was now running late.

He dashed out of his room, racing to the veranda, and then to the garden below the tree. His heart sank as he took in the scene before him. The flowers that were usually scattered on the ground were now neatly arranged in the shape of a heart, a final, poignant touch that spoke volumes. It was clear that the tribal girl had been there and had left in a way that seemed almost symbolic.

The sight of the heart-shaped arrangement filled Sanjay with a profound sense of loss and regret. The moment he had eagerly anticipated and prepared for had slipped through his fingers. The garden, once a place of hopeful dreams and unspoken words, now felt emptier than ever.

As he stood there, staring at the carefully arranged flowers, Sanjay's emotions swirled in a mix of disappointment and heartache. The tribal girl had gone, leaving behind a silent reminder of what could have been.

As Sanjay took his seat on the bus that day, bidding farewell to his parents, a heavy sadness settled over him. The dual weight of leaving his family and not having had a final chance to speak with the flower girl pressed down on him. His heart ached with the missed opportunity and the unresolved feelings he carried with him.

As the bus rumbled through the winding ghats, Sanjay's mind was consumed by regret. The picturesque landscape outside did little to lift his spirits; instead, it seemed to amplify his sense of loss. The lush, green hills and serene vistas contrasted sharply with the turmoil inside him. He cursed himself for not having taken the chance to express his feelings and for leaving without even knowing her name.

The journey felt interminable as he reflected on the fleeting moments he had shared with her. Each bend in the road seemed to echo his regret and longing. Sanjay's thoughts were a turbulent mix of sorrow and self-reproach. He was haunted by the unanswered questions and the "what ifs" of what could have been.

The bus's steady progress through the Sahyadri's only underscored his separation from the world he had briefly been part of. The vibrant memories of the flower girl and the garden were now distant and bittersweet echoes, fading with each mile. Sanjay's heart ached with the realisation that he had left behind something precious, a connection that had profoundly touched him but remained incomplete.

Sanjay never returned to the village after that fateful day. Two months later, his father received a transfer to Pune, marking the end of their time in the small town. This move unknowingly sealed Sanjay's departure from the place where his heart had been touched so profoundly.

The tribal girl remained a cherished memory, a poignant reminder of what could have been. Despite the passage of time, her image and the emotions he felt for her lingered in his heart. The missed opportunity became a lesson Sanjay carried with him throughout his life.

In reflecting on his experience, Sanjay realised the true cost of inaction and missed chances. The pain of not speaking up or making the effort when his heart urged him to, was a powerful lesson. He understood that many people find themselves unhappy not because they don't achieve their desires, but because they let crucial moments slip by, failing to seize the opportunities life presents.

Sanjay's experience taught him that the real tragedy lies in not taking action when it matters most – when the heart's desires align with the fleeting chances life offers. His story became a testament to the importance of courage and timing, and a reminder to embrace the moments when they arise, rather than letting them fade away into regret.

Back in the village, life continued its steady rhythm. The tree, ever ancient and wise, stands as a silent witness to the passage of time. Its branches still cradle the vibrant flowers that bloom with the same grace they always have, painting the ground with their delicate colours. The birds continue their melodies, their chirps weaving through the air like familiar, comforting notes. The wind's soothing whoosh maintains its rhythmic tune, a gentle reminder of the serene beauty of the village.

Though Sanjay's presence has long since faded from these hills, the essence of his experience remains intertwined with the landscape. The garden, the flowers, and the sounds of nature carry the echoes of his story, a testament to the fleeting yet profound moments that shape our lives. The village endures, with its timeless charm and the enduring cycles of nature, as if holding onto the memories of those who have come and gone.

In the quiet of the evening, as the sun dips below the horizon and casts a golden glow over the land, the tree stands as a monument to the ephemeral yet enduring connections we make. The flowers continue to bloom, the birds to sing, and the wind to whisper, a continuous celebration of life's simple, enduring beauty. And in these moments of stillness, the village holds within it the echoes of a young man's heart and the lessons learned from the fleeting dance of love and opportunity.

Chapter 2

Metal Trunk

In the heart of Devrukh stands the ancestral home of the Joshi family, a beautiful, old-fashioned house with a red-tiled roof and wooden pillars. This traditional Konkani-style house is a testament to the region's architectural heritage, with its spacious verandas, intricately carved wooden doors, and large, airy rooms. The house is surrounded by a lush garden where colourful flowers bloom, and the shade of ancient trees provides a cool respite from the sun.

Devrukh is a picturesque village nestled in the Konkan region of Maharashtra, India. It lies about 280 kilometres south of Mumbai and approximately 100 kilometres from the Arabian Sea. Devrukh is part of the Ratnagiri district, known for its lush green landscapes, serene environment, and rich cultural heritage.

The village of Devrukh is surrounded by the majestic mountain range, which provides a stunning backdrop of rolling hills and dense forests. The air is filled with the fragrance of blooming flowers and the chirping of birds, creating a symphony of nature that soothes the soul. The terrain is a delightful mix of valleys and gentle slopes, with winding roads that meander through fields and mango trees.

One of the most striking features of Devrukh is its abundance of mango, jackfruit, and coconut trees. The village is renowned for its Alphonso mangoes, which are considered some of the best in the world. During the mango season, the entire area is enveloped in the sweet, heady aroma of ripe mangoes. Jackfruit trees, with their large, spiky fruits, dot the landscape, adding to the village's verdant charm.

Devrukh's agricultural fields are a patchwork of vibrant greens and earthy browns, with crops like rice, groundnuts, and various vegetables thriving in the fertile soil. The villagers, who are mostly farmers, take great pride in their land and follow traditional farming practices that have been passed down through generations. The fields are bordered by well-maintained footpaths where one can often see farmers tending to their crops or carrying fresh produce to the local market.

The village's cultural life is vibrant and deeply rooted in tradition. Festivals like Ganesh Chaturthi, Diwali, and Holi are celebrated with great fervour, bringing the community together in joyous celebration. During these times, the village is adorned with lights, decorations, and the sounds of music and laughter fill the air. Traditional dance and music performances are a common sight, and the villagers don their finest attire to partake in the festivities.

Devrukh's beauty is not just in its physical landscape, but also in the simplicity and warmth of its people. The villagers are known for their hospitality, always ready to welcome guests with a smile and a cup of steaming hot tea. Their way of life is slow-paced and deeply connected to nature, offering a stark contrast to the hustle and bustle of city life.

As the sun sets over Devrukh, the sky is painted in hues of orange and pink, casting a golden glow over the village. The air cools down, and the stars begin to twinkle in the clear night sky. The sounds of the day fade away, replaced by the gentle hum of crickets and the distant call of night birds. It is in these tranquil moments that Devrukh reveals its true essence – a serene, beautiful village that embodies the harmony between man and nature.

Back in Pune, the Joshi family was super excited as they loaded their heavily packed bags into the trunk of their car. They had been planning for this trip from Pune to Devrukh, their native place, for the last 2-3 months, and the anticipation had been building up in their household. Shripad Joshi, his wife Manjiri, their elder daughter Richa, and their son Ganesh were all set to visit their native village. The children were particularly thrilled to visit their grandparents, whom they adored.

Shripad Joshi, a 45-year-old engineer with a calm demeanour and a thick moustache, was the head of the family. He had moved from his hometown to Pune for college and had settled there. Shripad was a man of principles, known for his disciplined lifestyle and love for his family. He wore glasses that gave him an intellectual look, and his eyes often sparkled with kindness and wisdom. His excitement for the trip was palpable as he double-checked the car's engine, ensuring everything was in perfect order for the long drive ahead.

Manjiri, his 42-year-old wife, was a homemaker known for her warm and nurturing nature. Her long, flowing hair was always neatly tied in a braid, and she wore traditional sarees that accentuated her graceful presence. Manjiri's excitement was evident in the way she meticulously packed homemade snacks and refreshments for the journey. She had a knack for making everyone feel loved and cared for, and her gentle smile was a constant source of comfort for her family.

Richa, their 14-year-old daughter, was an inquisitive teenager with a penchant for reading. Her spectacles often slid down her nose as she buried herself in books, and her love for literature had earned her the nickname "bookworm" at school. Richa had inherited her mother's looks and her father's calm demeanour. She was particularly excited about the trip because she planned to collect stories from her grandparents, hoping to weave them into her school essays and projects.

Ganesh, fondly called *'Ganu'*, was an energetic 8-year-old with a knack for asking endless questions. His large, curious eyes and perpetual smile made him the apple of everyone's eye. Ganu's excitement knew no bounds as he bounced around the car, eagerly talking about all the adventures he planned to have in Devrukh. His grandparents' house, with its sprawling garden and mysterious old attic, was his favourite place in the world.

As they finally set off, the car was filled with a mixture of laughter, chatter, and the occasional song from the radio. Shripad took the wheel, navigating through the early morning traffic of Pune, while Manjiri handed out sandwiches and homemade snacks. Richa had her nose in a book, occasionally looking up to point out interesting sights to her brother. Ganu, on the other hand, was glued to the window, marvelling at the changing landscape as they left the city behind and entered the countryside.

Every few miles, Ganu would burst out with a new question: "How much longer, Baba?" or "What kind of trees are those, Aai?" Shripad and Manjiri answered patiently, their own excitement mirrored in their children's eager faces. The journey, though long, was filled with a sense of togetherness and joy, each mile bringing them closer to the beloved village and the loving arms of Anant and Saraswati Joshi, Shripad's parents.

Shripad's parents, though they visited Pune once a year, had never left their hometown of Devrukh. The children knew the amount of love and pampering they would receive from their grandparents. They remembered past visits filled with stories, homemade treats, and the freedom to explore the vast, enchanting garden. The thought of these delights made the long journey seem shorter and the wait more bearable.

As they neared Devrukh, the familiar sights of lush greenery, winding roads, and the distant hills brought a wave of nostalgia to Shripad. He recalled his own childhood, running through the same fields, climbing the same trees, and listening to his father's tales under the starlit sky. It felt like a homecoming, not just to a place, but to a time filled with love and warmth.

The car's tyres crunched on the gravel path leading to their ancestral home, a beautiful, old-fashioned house with a red-tiled roof and wooden pillars. Anant and Saraswati were already waiting on the veranda, their faces lighting up with joy as they saw the car approaching. The moment the car came to a halt, Ganu and Richa leaped out and ran to their grandparents, their laughter echoing through the serene evening air.

"Ganu," Saraswati called him into the kitchen with a warm smile. The grandparents fondly called Ganesh "Ganu," a name that carried with it layers of affection and nostalgia. As Ganu entered the kitchen, his eyes widened at the sight of a freshly cut pineapple, glistening with juicy sweetness. Saraswati, his grandmother, had cut it just for him, knowing how much he loved the tropical fruit.

"Aajji, why were you crying when you hugged me?" Ganu asked, his voice filled with innocent curiosity. His big, inquisitive eyes looked up at her, searching for an answer. Saraswati, taken aback by the directness of his question, felt a lump in her throat. How could she possibly explain the rush of emotions that had overwhelmed her?

Saraswati had seen her son Shripad in Ganu's eyes, his smile, and his curious nature. Ganu was the spitting image of Shripad when he was a child, and every time she looked at her grandson, it was like looking back in time. Memories of Shripad's childhood flooded her mind – his first steps, his first words, the way he used to run around the house laughing. Those were precious moments she cherished deeply.

Unable to find the right words to convey her feelings to a child, she simply knelt down and hugged Ganu tightly. The warmth of his small body, the scent of his hair, and the sound of his heartbeat brought a sense of peace to her. "Some feelings are too big for words, my dear," she whispered softly, her voice trembling with emotion.

Ganu, feeling the depth of his grandmother's love, hugged her back just as tightly. Though he didn't fully understand why she was crying, he could sense the love and care in her embrace. It made him feel safe and cherished.

After a few moments, Saraswati pulled back, wiped a tear from her cheek, and smiled at Ganu. "You remind me so much of your father when he was your age," she said, her eyes twinkling with a mixture of sadness and joy. "It's like seeing him grow up all over again."

Ganu nodded, accepting her explanation in his childlike way. He picked up a piece of pineapple and took a bite, savouring its sweetness. As he did, he felt a deeper connection to his grandmother, sensing that their bond was rooted in something profound and timeless.

Saraswati watched him eat, her heart swelling with love. She felt grateful for these moments, for the chance to see her family's legacy continue through Ganu. The kitchen, filled with the aroma of fresh fruit and the warmth of shared love, seemed like the heart of their home – a place where past, present, and future came together in a beautiful, harmonious dance.

At 9:00 PM, Shripad interrupted Ganu's endless stream of questions and excitement. "Come on, Ganu, it's time for bed," he said gently but firmly. Shripad, visibly tired from the long day and the drive, was eager to get some rest himself. He picked up his son, who was still buzzing with energy and excitement, and carried him towards the bedroom.

Ganu protested, "But Baba, I'm not sleepy yet!" His eyes, however, were already starting to droop, betraying his words.

Sensing his grandson's reluctance to end the day, Grandfather Anant stepped in with a reassuring smile. "Shripad, let me take Ganu to bed tonight," he offered, his voice soothing and calm. "I have some stories that might just help him fall asleep,"

Shripad, grateful for the offer and trusting his father's ability to handle Ganu's boundless energy, nodded. "Alright, Baba! Good night." he said. He gave Ganu a kiss on the forehead before heading to his own room, where Manjiri was already settling in for the night.

Ganu, now in his grandfather's comforting embrace, felt a wave of calm wash over him. Anant carried him to his and Saraswati's bedroom, a room filled with the nostalgic aroma of aged wood, old books, and the faint scent of sandalwood incense. The bed was tucked in one corner, opposite a window that overlooked the moonlit garden. Marathi books and novels were stacked on a small table beside a large, old radio that added to the room's rustic charm.

The walls were adorned with photographs of the family through the years – from Shripad's childhood to the present day. Ganu's eyes wandered over the pictures, fascinated by the snippets of history captured in each frame.

As he continued to explore the room with his eyes, he noticed a large, old metal trunk hidden under the bed. It was worn and rusty.

"Ajoba, what's in that trunk?" Ganu asked, his curiosity piqued.

Anant chuckled, a twinkle in his eye. "Ah, that trunk belonged to your great-grandfather, Ganeshrao Bandopant Joshi. It contains some of his most cherished possessions. I've kept it safe all these years."

Ganu's eyes widened with curiosity and excitement. "Can we open it, Ajoba? Please?"

Anant smiled and patted Ganu's head. "Not tonight, Ganu. It's late, and you need to sleep. But I promise, I'll tell you all about your great-grandfather and what's in that trunk tomorrow. How does that sound?"

Ganu, although still eager, was beginning to feel the day's adventures catching up to him. "Okay, Ajoba, tomorrow then."

Anant tucked Ganu into bed, pulling the soft, old quilt up to his chin. He sang a gentle lullaby, a tune that had been passed down through generations, and within minutes, Ganu was fast asleep, his little chest rising and falling with each peaceful breath. Anant kissed his grandson on the forehead, his heart full of love and nostalgia.

As he turned to look at Saraswati, who was resting on her rocking chair, their eyes met, both glistening with unshed tears. They smiled at each other, silently acknowledging the preciousness of these moments and the continuity of their family's legacy. Finally, they settled down for the night, comforted by the presence of their loved ones and the quiet serenity of their home.

Shripad had woken up early, the first light of dawn just beginning to filter through the trees. He stepped outside to the fresh, crisp morning air and found his father, Anant, already in the garden, tending to the trees. The garden was a lush oasis of greenery, with tall mango and jackfruit trees casting dappled shadows on the ground. The scent of wet earth and blooming flowers filled the air, and the gentle rustling of leaves provided a soothing soundtrack.

Anant was inspecting the trees with a practiced eye, his hands gently touching the leaves and branches, checking for any signs of damage. Shripad joined him, and together they strolled through the garden, side by side. As they walked, they fell into an easy conversation, their words flowing naturally like the streams that meandered through the village.

"How have you been, Baba? How's your health?" Shripad asked, his voice filled with genuine concern.

"I'm doing well, Shripad," Anant replied with a reassuring smile. "The usual aches and pains of old age, but nothing to worry about. How about you? How is work treating you?"

Shripad sighed, a hint of weariness in his voice. "Work is hectic, but I manage. It's always good to come back here, though. It reminds me of simpler times."

Anant nodded, understanding. "Yes, time spent with family is precious. It gives us strength and reminds us of what truly matters."

Meanwhile, inside the house, Saraswati and Manjiri were busy in the kitchen. The kitchen was a hive of activity, filled with the clattering of pots and pans, the sizzle of spices being fried, and the rich aroma of traditional Konkani dishes. Saraswati, ever the diligent matriarch, was instructing Manjiri on where things were kept and how to prepare certain dishes that had been family favourites for generations.

"Manjiri, the masala box is in the top cupboard, and the rice is in the large container by the window," Saraswati said, her voice kind but firm. "And don't forget to add the special spice mix to the curry. It's what gives it that unique flavour."

Manjiri nodded, absorbing every bit of information. She loved these moments, learning from Saraswati and bonding over shared recipes and stories. The kitchen, with its warmth and aroma, felt like the heart of the home, a place where traditions were kept alive and passed down.

As the morning progressed, Ganu woke up, rubbing his eyes and stretching. He could hear the soft murmur of voices and the comforting sounds of home. With a yawn, he got out of bed and made his way to the garden where he saw his father and grandfather walking among the trees. His face lit up with a bright smile, and he ran towards them, his small feet padding softly on the dewy grass.

"Ajoba!" Ganu called out, his voice filled with joy.

Anant turned, his face breaking into a wide smile as he saw his grandson running towards him. He bent down, albeit with some difficulty, and scooped Ganu up into his arms. Ganu laid his head on his grandfather's shoulder, feeling the strong, familiar embrace that always made him feel safe.

"Good morning, Ganu," Anant said, kissing the top of his head. "Did you sleep well?"

Ganu nodded, his eyes still heavy with sleep. He stayed quiet, content to simply be in his grandfather's arms as Anant and Shripad continued their inspection of the garden. The tranquillity of the morning, the soft rustle of leaves, and the presence of his family made Ganu feel at peace.

As they finished their walk and returned to the veranda, Ganu whispered in his grandfather's ear, "Ajoba, story?"

Anant chuckled softly and kissed Ganu's cheek. "Of course, Ganu. Let's sit down and I'll tell you all about your great-grandfather and the treasures in his old trunk."

They settled into the veranda, the morning sun casting a golden glow around them. Ganu snuggled into his grandfather's lap, eager and ready to listen to the stories of the past.

They sat, and grandfather related the story:

Ganeshrao Bandopant Joshi, fondly known as Joshi Kaka, was a man of multifaceted personality, deeply respected in Devrukh and beyond. His physical presence was imposing, but it was his character that truly set him apart.

Ganeshrao stood tall at six foot two, with a rugged, muscular build that spoke of years of hard work and discipline. His attire was always immaculate, favouring a neatly tucked dhoti and kurta, paired with an uparna draped elegantly over his shoulder and a traditional pheta on his head. His sharply turned-up moustache and piercing eyes added to his authoritative appearance, making him a figure that commanded both respect and admiration.

Ganeshrao was a man who valued discipline above all else. His life was governed by a strict adherence to routines and schedules. He believed that time was a precious resource that should never be wasted, a belief symbolised by his cherished HMT watch. This watch was more than a timepiece; it was a constant reminder of the importance of managing time effectively.

As a prominent mango trader, Ganeshrao built his reputation on the pillars of integrity and fairness. He was known for his honesty in business dealings, ensuring that farmers in Devrukh received fair prices for their produce. His commitment to fairness extended to all aspects of his life, making him a trusted figure in the community.

Ganeshrao was a man of deep thought and introspection. He maintained a daily personal diary, documenting his reflections, learnings, and the events of each day. This habit of journaling not only helped him stay organised but also provided a medium for self-improvement and wisdom sharing. His diaries were a treasure trove of insights, filled with lessons on life, business, and morality.

His strong baritone voice and commanding presence made Ganeshrao a natural leader. He was often sought after for advice and guidance, whether it was for personal matters or community issues. His leadership was marked by a balance of firmness and compassion, making him both respected and loved by those who knew him.

Despite his stern exterior, Ganeshrao had a heart full of compassion. He was generous with his wealth and time, always willing to help those in need. He believed in uplifting others and was known for his charitable deeds in Devrukh. His home was always open to guests, and his hospitality was legendary.

Ganeshrao placed immense value on education. He ensured that his children received the best education possible, believing that knowledge was the key to a better life. He encouraged them to be curious, ethical, and respectful of others, regardless of their social standing. His emphasis on education was not just academic, but also moral, aiming to produce well-rounded, enlightened individuals.

Ganeshrao's relationships were marked by a deep sense of responsibility and care. As a husband, he was supportive and loving, ensuring his wife felt valued and respected. As a father, he was both a mentor and a guide, instilling in his children the values he held dear.

Ganeshrao's legacy was one of integrity, wisdom and compassion. His life and values continued to influence his descendants, guiding them in their actions and decisions. The old metal trunk under the bed, containing his cherished possessions, was a symbol of the enduring impact he had on his family. Through the stories told by Anant, Ganeshrao's spirit lived on, inspiring young Ganu and future generations to uphold the principles he held dear.

Ganeshrao Bandopant Joshi's HMT watch was a cherished symbol of his disciplined and meticulous nature. The watch featured a clean, white dial with bold black devnagri numerals, three sleek black hands, and a subtle texture that lent it a refined appearance. The round stainless steel case, polished to a high shine, housed a domed acrylic crystal that protected the dial and maintained its pristine look over the years. The small, ridged crown, embossed with the HMT logo, facilitated daily winding, a ritual Ganeshrao performed with care, reflecting his respect for time. The watch's mechanical hand-winding movement was a hallmark of HMT's traditional craftsmanship. Its brown leather strap, with a classic buckle clasp, aged gracefully, adding character to the watch. Ganeshrao wore this watch every day, considering it an essential part of his attire. It symbolised his belief in the importance of punctuality, diligence, and respect for others' time. The act of winding the watch each morning was a meditative practice connecting him to the rhythm of life and the passage of time. After his passing, the watch was preserved in an old metal trunk, becoming a cherished heirloom.

The story ends.

Ganu listened intently to the whole story, his young mind traversing the finer details of his great-grandfather's life as narrated by his grandfather. He imagined Ganeshrao's towering figure, his commanding presence, and the disciplined life he led. While everyone sat on the veranda chatting over tea and morning snacks, Ganu's curiosity got the better of him. He quietly slipped away and walked into his grandfather's room. He made his way to the bed and peered underneath it, spotting the old metal trunk that had captured his imagination. Determined to uncover its secrets, he pulled at the trunk, using all his strength to drag it out into the open.

The trunk was heavy, its surface worn and scratched from years of use. Ganu's small hands fumbled, but he eventually managed to open it. Inside, the treasures of Ganeshrao's life lay neatly arranged. The first thing Ganu saw was the pheta, its rich fabric still vibrant, evoking images of his great-grandfather wearing it with pride. Next to it was the HMT watch, gleaming softly in the light, exactly how it was described, a symbol of the disciplined life Ganeshrao led.

Ganu carefully lifted the diaries, their leather covers smooth and worn from years of handling. He opened one and marvelled at the calligraphic Marathi script, the ink still bold on the yellowing pages. He flipped through the diary, catching glimpses of Ganeshrao's thoughts, reflections, and daily experiences.

As Ganu explored the contents of the trunk, he felt a deep connection to the past. The items in the trunk were not just relics; they were pieces of a life well-lived, symbols of a legacy that now belonged to him. He carefully placed everything back in the trunk, except for the watch. Ganu took the watch in his hand, winding it gently. The watch started ticking, and with each tick, Ganu felt a sense of his great-grandfather's presence.

"Time is the key to life; you must respect it," a strong baritone voice echoed!

A shiver coursed through Ganu's spine. He could feel the imposing presence of his great-grandfather enveloping him. With reverence, he fastened the watch to his left wrist, the strap hanging a bit loose. Without hesitation, he rushed to the veranda, propelled by a mix of fear and excitement.

On the veranda sat a towering figure on a rocking chair. The man wore a majestic pheta, his moustache curling with an air of authority and pride.

Ganu paused for a moment, taking in the sight, his heart pounding. The air felt charged, almost electric. Gathering his courage, he stepped forward, his eyes locked on the figure before him. The old man seemed to radiate a warmth that contrasted sharply with his formidable appearance.

Ganu's steps quickened, his initial apprehension melting away into a deep sense of connection and respect. As he reached the rocking chair, he felt a surge of emotions, a blend of awe and reverence, for the man who had left such an indelible mark on their family.

Anant hugged him. For a moment, Ganu felt that his great-grandfather was alive!

Chapter 3

Panchgani Escapade

"What the hell is this?" Smruti remarked irritably, looking at her husband.

The relationship between Smruti and Rushikesh had soured over the last two years, casting a shadow over what was once a vibrant and loving partnership. They had been married for five years, a journey that began with boundless hope and excitement. Their story started over a decade ago when they first met during their freshman year in engineering college. From late-night study sessions to shared dreams of the future, they built a bond that felt unbreakable. Against the wishes of both their parents, who had different expectations and reservations, they decided to marry. Back then, they were confident that love would conquer all, not foreseeing the challenges that lay ahead.

Smruti, a striking woman from Andheri, a suburb in Mumbai, possessed a beauty that turned heads wherever she went. Standing tall with sharp, distinguished features, she could easily be mistaken for an air hostess. Her curly hair, now straightened, was always meticulously styled, giving her face an open, captivating look that drew people in. Her eyebrows, neatly trimmed and sharply defined, framed her expressive, round eyes which were accentuated by a touch of kajal, enhancing their natural allure. Her sharp jawline added to her elegance, and her thin lips, when she smiled, had a way of making hearts skip a beat.

Smruti's fashion sense was impeccable. She was always dressed to perfection, with an acute sense of style and a meticulous approach to her appearance. Her presence commanded attention and admiration, a reflection of her inner confidence and strength.

Growing up in Andheri's Four Bungalows, Smruti was the daughter of an Air India pilot. Her childhood was filled with the comforts and luxuries of an affluent life. She enjoyed the delights of chocolates from abroad, pretty dresses, and the security of a stable, loving home. Her father, who had dedicated his life to the skies, ensured that his family never lacked for anything. Smruti's mother, a graceful and supportive woman, nurtured her daughter's ambitions and dreams. This privileged upbringing gave her a plethora of choices and the freedom to carve her own path, whether it was in her career or her choice of a partner.

From a young age, Smruti was fiercely independent with a unique perspective on life. She was a curious and intelligent child, always eager to learn and explore new things. Her confidence and strong will were evident in everything she did, making her stand out in any crowd. She excelled academically and participated in various extracurricular activities, from debating to dance, showcasing her diverse talents. Her parents' support and the opportunities afforded by her upbringing enabled her to dream big and pursue her goals with determination.

When she met Rushikesh in college, it was a meeting of minds and hearts. Rushikesh was drawn to Smruti's intelligence, charm, and beauty, while Smruti admired Rushikesh's dedication, kindness, and sense of humour. Their relationship blossomed quickly, and they became inseparable. They shared a passion for learning and a vision for the future, often discussing their dreams and aspirations late into the night. Despite the initial resistance from their families, they stood firm in their decision to be together, believing that their love was strong enough to overcome any obstacle.

Their wedding was a beautiful celebration of love, filled with joy, laughter, and the promise of a bright future. The first few years of marriage were blissful, marked by shared adventures, mutual support, and the excitement of building a life together. They travelled, explored new places, and created cherished memories. They supported each other's careers and celebrated each other's successes. However, as time went on, the pressures of life began to take their toll. Work stress, family expectations, and personal ambitions started to create cracks in their relationship. The communication that once flowed so easily between them began to falter, and misunderstandings grew more frequent.

Smruti's career demands often required long hours and travel, while Rushikesh's own professional responsibilities left him with little time to nurture their relationship. They found themselves drifting apart, caught up in their own worlds and struggling to find common ground. The vibrant connection they once shared began to fade, replaced by silence and resentment. They tried to bridge the gap, but the unresolved issues and unspoken grievances kept widening the distance between them.

Their home, which was once filled with laughter and love, became a battleground of unspoken tensions and unmet expectations.

In the quiet moments, Smruti often found herself reflecting on their journey, wondering where things had gone wrong. She missed the closeness they once shared, the comfort of knowing that Rushikesh was her rock and her confidant. She longed for the days when they could talk for hours about anything and everything, when their love felt invincible. Yet, despite her longing, she struggled to find a way back to that place of connection and understanding. The weight of their unspoken grievances and the pressures of their individual lives created a barrier that seemed insurmountable.

Rushikesh, too, felt the strain of their deteriorating relationship. He missed the warmth and companionship of Smruti, the joy of their shared dreams, and the comfort of their love. He often found himself replaying their happiest moments, yearning for the simplicity and joy they once knew. But, like Smruti, he was at a loss for how to bridge the growing chasm between them. The more they tried to mend their relationship, the more their efforts seemed to fall short, leaving them both feeling frustrated and disheartened.

As they navigated this challenging phase of their marriage, Smruti and Rushikesh were forced to confront their individual and collective issues. They had to grapple with their unmet expectations, their unfulfilled desires, and the evolving dynamics of their relationship. It was a time of introspection and reflection, a period that tested their resilience and their commitment to each other. In the end, their journey would depend on their ability to rediscover the love and connection that had brought them together in the first place and to rebuild their relationship on a foundation of mutual understanding, respect, and love.

Eager to make amends and restore their once amicable life, Rushikesh made a plan.

"Hey Smruti... eh... I was thinking... if... if we could go to Panchgani over the weekend and relive the good old days!" Rushikesh asked Smruti in the morning as she was hurrying to get to her office.

It was Monday, and she had her monthly board meeting. Without answering, she dashed out of the door. Rushikesh could hear the car zooming out of their porch. Silence engulfed the room, and his mind diverted to his work that lay ahead.

Rushikesh seemed lost the whole day. When suddenly, around 4:00 PM, he got a text message from Smruti.

"Yes, we can. Thanks for asking!" Smruti had replied.

He smiled and was glad that he made that effort to ask. Smruti kept thinking about what her husband had asked while zooming to her office.

"Where are we staying?" asked Smruti as they were packing their individual bags for the weekend trip tomorrow.

"Parsi Cottage," replied Rushikesh.

"Ah," sighed Smruti, who thought that this may be the lamest choice her husband had made. However, she did not react. She was looking forward to the trip, and the place really did not matter. Though a thought of the place crossed her mind.

Parsi Cottage was an old villa situated in Panchgani, near Mahabaleshwar, tucked away from the bustling town and nestled amidst the serene beauty of the Western Ghats. One had to take a left from the bus stand, following a winding road that led up to the hillock. Built in 1885 by a Parsi family, the house exuded an old-world charm, with British architectural influences seeping into its design. The generations had taken great care of the house, preserving its historical essence while maintaining its functionality.

The exterior of Parsi Cottage was a sight to behold. Ivy climbed up the stone walls, giving it a rustic and timeless look. The structure stood tall with its weathered brickwork, white-framed windows, and a gabled roof adorned with terracotta tiles. The front porch, supported by intricately carved wooden pillars, welcomed guests with an air of vintage elegance. The sprawling gardens surrounding the cottage were a riot of colours, with manicured lawns and vibrant flower beds. Roses, marigolds, and bougainvillea bloomed in profusion, filling the air with their sweet fragrances.

The cottage was surrounded by tall trees that provided shade and a sense of seclusion. The path leading to the entrance was lined with cobblestones, and an old wrought-iron gate marked the entrance to the property. As they drove through the gate, the crunch of gravel under the tyres added to the sense of stepping back in time. Birds chirped in the trees, and the gentle rustling of leaves created a soothing symphony.

Inside, Parsi Cottage was just as enchanting. The foyer opened into a spacious living area with high ceilings and large windows that let in ample natural light. The walls were adorned with vintage paintings and photographs, each telling a story of the house's rich history. Antique furniture pieces, carefully chosen and well-preserved, were arranged tastefully throughout the rooms. The living room had a cosy fireplace, its mantle decorated with trinkets and memorabilia from a bygone era. Plush sofas and armchairs invited guests to sit and relax, offering a perfect blend of comfort and elegance.

The dining room was another marvel, with a long wooden table that could easily seat a large family. The chairs, upholstered in rich fabric, were as comfortable as they were beautiful. An ornate chandelier hung from the ceiling, casting a warm, inviting glow over the room. The sideboard was laden with fine china and silverware, ready for any occasion. French doors opened out onto a veranda that overlooked the valley, providing a stunning view of the surrounding hills and forests.

Their room was located on the ground floor, overlooking a gorgeous valley lined with a range of mountains. The air breezed through the windows swiftly. The room was well-decorated with elegant paintings on the walls, a huge wardrobe in one corner, and a large bed. The bed looked royal with its premium bedding and curtains. The gracious charm of the room oozed with antiqueness and royalty. Next to the window stood a huge study table. One could overlook the valley while sitting at the table. The study table was a masterpiece of craftsmanship, made from rich mahogany and polished to a high sheen. Its surface was smooth and cool to the touch, with intricate carvings along the edges that spoke of its vintage elegance. The drawers, fitted with brass handles, promised to hold secrets of the past, and the very sight of it evoked a sense of history and grandeur.

The bathroom, though modernised for comfort, retained an old-world charm with its clawfoot bathtub and vintage fixtures. The tiles were a mix of classic black and white, and the large mirror had an ornate frame that added to the room's elegance.

The veranda, which wrapped around the cottage, was a perfect spot to enjoy the tranquil surroundings. Wooden rocking chairs and a swing bench provided comfortable seating options, while small tables were perfect for holding a cup of tea or a book. The view from the veranda was nothing short of spectacular, with the valley stretching out below and the mountains rising majestically in the distance. The fresh, cool breeze carried the scents of pine and flowers, making it a perfect spot to relax and rejuvenate.

Parsi Cottage, with its blend of historical charm and natural beauty, provided the perfect backdrop for Rushikesh's and Smruti's attempt to rekindle their relationship. It was a place where time seemed to stand still, allowing them to reflect on their past and look forward to their future.

Their dinner at Parsi Cottage was a delightful journey through the rich and aromatic world of Parsi cuisine. The dining room was an elegant space with a long wooden table that could accommodate a large gathering. The table was set with fine china, silverware and sparkling glassware, ready for a sumptuous feast. The chandelier above cast a warm glow, illuminating the room and creating an inviting atmosphere.

The menu for the evening featured a variety of traditional Parsi dishes, each prepared with care and attention to detail. The aromas wafting from the kitchen hinted at the culinary delights to come, making their mouths water in anticipation.

The table was laden with these delicacies, each dish tempting. The vibrant colours, enticing aromas, and rich flavours of the Parsi cuisine created a feast for the senses. Smruti and Rushikesh ate in relative silence, both engrossed in the culinary experience. The food brought back memories of happier times, shared meals, and the warmth of family gatherings.

After dinner, both went to their room. Rushikesh lit a lamp on the study table and sat looking at the dark sky that adorned the visible stars. Smruti was tired, and she slept thinking she would make the most of the 2 days that lay ahead of them. She was happy to have taken this trip. In about two minutes, she was in deep slumber.

As Rushikesh looked at the pitch-dark sky, stars shining bright, he thought of where life had come to. What happened to the love that knew no bounds? He opened the drawer of the antique mahogany table, crafted to perfection, and saw blank letterheads. The black fountain pen caught his attention. The pen was an exquisite piece, its body made of glossy black lacquer with gold trimmings. It had a weight to it that felt substantial and reassuring in his hand. The nib, fine and precise, gleamed under the lamp's light, promising to flow smoothly and effortlessly across the page.

Rushikesh pulled out a letterhead, opened the pen, and started writing.

Dear Smruti,

I love you. I always will...

He kept on thinking about the cherished memories and the time they had loved each other. He continued writing the letter, thinking in between, smiling, and then worried.

The wall clock was showing a perfect five in the morning. Little did Rushikesh realise how the time flew by. He signed the letter, put it in an envelope, and wrote 'To my Love - Smruti'.

The sky was getting brighter. The birds had started chirping, and the valley looked as if it was alive, ready to dance. He put on his jacket and left the room to take a walk around.

Smruti woke up to the chirping noises of the birds. She extended her hand to find Rushikesh, but he was not there. She realised he had never slept as the other part of the bed remained untouched. Upon waking up, she noticed Rushikesh was not in the room and assumed he might have gone out for a walk. Her eyes fell on the envelope with her name on the table. She opened the envelope and started reading.

Dear Smruti,

I hate you. I always will. You are the biggest mistake of my life. I wonder, the forsaken day I met you...

Tears rolled out from Smruti's eyes; her heart broke as she continued reading the letter. She did not realise to what end her love had come. She hated herself for getting her relationship to this state. She was not angry with Rushikesh, but she could understand his pain and why their life was now strained.

She dropped the letter on the table, put on her gown, and rushed to the veranda. She could see Rushikesh facing the valley, lost in his own thoughts as the wind ruffled his hair. She ran and hugged him tightly from behind.

"Rushikesh, I love you, and I am deeply sorry," she said.

Rushikesh did not utter a word. He turned and held Smruti tightly in his arms, feeling the same way he had hugged her for the first time. They did not speak a word, but deep down, they knew that they had passed the test of life, and love had won the test of time.

In the drawer of the mahogany table in their room, the antique fountain pen smiled. The pen had completely reversed Rushikesh's letter. The letter surely jolted Smruti. Little did Rushikesh know what had happened, nor did Smruti. Once again, the fountain pen had successfully restored the lost love.

Chapter 4

Radha's Morning Companions

As Sudhakar sat in his favourite rocking chair on the balcony of his apartment, the gentle creaking of the wood seemed to blend with the soft patter of rain against the balcony. His gaze, though fixed on the drizzling rain, was far away, lost in the labyrinth of memories that had accumulated over 75 years. The rain, a constant companion through the seasons of his life, always had a way of drawing him back into reflection.

He remembered his passing parade vividly – a moment frozen in time. The crisp uniform, the polished boots, the weight of the rifle in his hands, and the surge of pride as he marched in perfect sync with his fellow cadets. At just 20 years old, he was stepping into a life that would demand everything from him. The rigorous training, the sleepless nights, the bonds forged in the crucible of discipline and duty – they were all as fresh in his mind as if they had happened yesterday.

The army had been his life, a life that had taken him across the country and beyond. He had served in various roles, each one demanding, and each one shaping him into the man he had become. He had known the taste of victory and the sting of loss, had witnessed bravery and sacrifice, had led men into situations where the outcome was uncertain. Through it all, he had remained steadfast, driven by a sense of duty that had been instilled in him from that very first day at the NDA.

When he returned to the NDA as a Senior Instructor in the final years of his career, it felt like coming full circle. The academy had changed, but the essence of it remained the same—the relentless pursuit of excellence, the forging of character, the preparation of young men to face the challenges that lay ahead. As a Senior Instructor, he was not just a teacher but a mentor, a figure of authority and respect, someone the cadets looked up to. He took pride in moulding the next generation, passing on the wisdom he had gained through decades of service.

Even after his retirement, Sudhakar's bond with the NDA remained unbroken. He would still make it a point to attend the passing out parades, standing tall among the sea of young faces, his presence a silent testament to a life dedicated to service. Watching the new cadets march, he saw in them the same fire and determination that had driven him all those years ago. It was a connection to his past, a reassurance that the values he had lived by were still being carried forward.

Now, as he sat in his rocking chair, the rain a constant whisper, Sudhakar felt a deep sense of contentment. His life had been one of purpose and fulfilment, and the memories he carried were a source of comfort. They were not just memories of battles fought or medals won, but of a life lived with honour, a life that had made a difference. As the rain continued to fall, Sudhakar closed his eyes, letting the memories wash over him like the rain washing over the earth, nourishing and renewing, a reminder that every moment had been worth it.

After retiring, Sudhakar and Radha, his wife, chose to settle in Pune, a city that held a special place in their hearts. Pune offered a peaceful respite from the years of constant movement that had defined their lives. For Radha, it was a return to the familiar, a city she had often thought of as home, even amidst the many places they had lived.

Radha had been the anchor in Sudhakar's life, accompanying him through every transfer and every challenge that his military career threw their way. As a dedicated teacher, she found ways to continue her passion, no matter where they were stationed. Whether in a remote town or a bustling city, Radha would find a school and immerse herself in teaching. She had an innate ability to connect with children, and her presence in the classroom brought a sense of continuity and purpose to their often-transient life.

Their marriage was a partnership built on mutual respect and understanding. Through the years, they had faced the uncertainties of military life together – the long separations, the ever-present risks, and the constant need to adapt to new environments. Radha's unwavering support had been a source of strength for Sudhakar, allowing him to focus on his duties, with the knowledge that his family was well taken care of.

Their daughter, who had inherited her mother's resilience and independence, had found her own path. She had married an IT professional and moved to the USA where she was now settled and thriving. Though miles apart, the bond between them remained strong, strengthened by regular calls and yearly visits. Sudhakar and Radha were proud of the life she had built for herself, and they were content knowing she was happy.

Their son, Suyog, had followed in his father's footsteps, choosing a career in the army. Sudhakar saw a lot of himself in Suyog – the same determination, the same sense of duty. Suyog was currently posted in Jaipur, where he lived with his wife and children. Sudhakar took great pride in his son's achievements and felt a deep connection with him, knowing that Suyog understood the life he had led, the sacrifices, and the rewards of serving the nation.

Pune became their sanctuary, a place where they could enjoy the slower pace of life while remaining connected to the family they had built. Radha continued to teach occasionally, finding joy in sharing her knowledge and experience with young minds. Sudhakar, on the other hand, enjoyed the calm of his days, often reflecting on the journey that had brought them here.

As they grew older, the love and companionship between Sudhakar and Radha deepened. They found comfort in their routines, in the simple pleasures of daily life, and in the knowledge that they had weathered the storms together. Their home in Pune became a gathering place for their children and grandchildren, a place filled with laughter, stories, and mostly memories of a life well-lived.

"Sudhakar!" Radha's voice, though soft, carried the familiar warmth and affection that had always been a part of their relationship. The sound of her voice pulled him out of his reverie, snapping the thread of memories that had been playing in his mind like an old, cherished movie. He gently placed his cup of tea on the small table beside his chair and got up.

"Could you take me to the bathroom?" Radha asked, her voice laced with a mixture of patience and frustration. It wasn't easy for her to ask for help, but these past two months had changed things.

"Of course, my darling Radha!" Sudhakar responded with the same gentle tone he always used when speaking to her, a tone that conveyed not just love, but deep respect and care. He moved to her side, helping her out of the bed with a tenderness that only years of companionship could cultivate.

Radha had been bedridden since her hip surgery, a result of a nasty fall that had shaken their world. The surgery had gone well, but the recovery was slow and gruelling. Sudhakar had taken it upon himself to be her primary caregiver, ensuring she was as comfortable as possible. He knew how fiercely independent Radha was, and he admired the quiet strength she showed, even now. But seeing her struggle, confined to bed, was heart-wrenching.

As he helped her to the bathroom, his grip on her was firm but gentle, supporting her every step of the way. This routine had become part of their daily life, a new chapter in their journey together. But to Sudhakar, it was not a burden; it was an extension of the love and care they had always shared. Radha had stood by him through the toughest times of his career, and now it was his turn to stand by her.

Once Radha was settled, Sudhakar returned to his rocking chair, but his thoughts were no longer as light as they had been. His mind wandered back to the vibrant woman Radha had been—always active, always involved in something, whether it was her teaching or managing their home. She had been his pillar, the one who kept everything together while he was away on duty. And now, seeing her in this state, dependent on him for the simplest tasks weighed heavily on his heart.

He couldn't help but worry about her recovery. The doctors had assured them that with time and therapy, she would regain her mobility, but Sudhakar knew how fragile things could be at their age. The thought of anything happening to Radha was unbearable and it gnawed at him constantly.

As he sat in his chair again, his thoughts drifted back to the life they had built together. The years of moving from one posting to another, the homes they had made in each new city, and the countless memories they had created along the way. He remembered their laughter, their shared challenges, and the quiet moments of togetherness that had made their life a wonderful journey.

These memories were his refuge now, a way to remind himself of the strength they both had. He knew that just as they had faced every other challenge in their lives together, they would get through this one too. But even with that resolve, the worry remained, a constant companion to the love and care he poured into every small task he did for her.

Sudhakar sighed softly, his heart heavy yet full of love. He would do everything in his power to help Radha recover, just as she had always done for him. For now, he would be her strength, just as she had been his for so many years.

Sudhakar's memories of that night at the RSI Club were vivid, a cherished moment etched in his mind with a clarity that defied the passage of time. It was a special evening, marking the end of an era and the beginning of a new chapter for him and his fellow cadets. The room buzzed with the excitement and nervous energy of young officers who were about to embark on their military careers. Among them, Sudhakar stood with his two closest mates, each of them recently commissioned and freshly assigned to the Gorkha regiment in the North East – a prestigious and challenging posting that they were eager to take on.

The dinner was a grand affair, attended by many high-ranking officers and their families. Among the most distinguished guests was Colonel Divakar Deshpande, a man whose reputation preceded him. Colonel Deshpande was an eminent figure at the NDA, known for his exemplary service and towering presence, both literally and figuratively. His tall, commanding stature was complemented by his impeccably groomed appearance. Even in his later years, he remained strikingly handsome, with a sharp jawline accentuated by an astounding moustache—thick, perfectly shaped, and a hallmark of his personality. His eyes, though warm, carried a certain intensity, a reflection of the life he had led.

His voice, deep and resonant, had the power to command attention effortlessly, cutting through the hum of conversation in the room. Yet, despite his formidable presence, Colonel Deshpande was known for his jovial nature. He had a way of making people feel at ease, whether it was a young cadet or a fellow officer. He was approachable, a man who could balance the seriousness of his duties with a light-heartedness that made him beloved by many.

As Sudhakar approached the bar counter to pick up his glass of whiskey, he heard his name being called in that unmistakable voice. He turned to see Colonel Deshpande walking towards him, a friendly smile on his face. Beside him was a young woman who immediately caught Sudhakar's eye. She was elegant, with an air of quiet confidence that seemed to mirror her father's.

Her name was Radha. Sudhakar would later come to know her as the woman who would become the centre of his world.

"Ah, Sudhakar! I've heard good things about you," Colonel Deshpande began, extending his hand in a firm handshake. "I'm Colonel Divakar Deshpande, and this is my daughter, Radha."

Sudhakar was struck by the Colonel's warmth. Despite his high rank and the authority he commanded, there was a genuine interest in his tone, a sense that this was more than just a formal introduction. As they spoke, Colonel Deshpande asked Sudhakar about his family, his background, and most intriguingly, his approach to life. The Colonel's questions were not mere small talk; they were probing, thoughtful, designed to understand the young officer's character and values.

Radha stood by her father's side, listening quietly, her eyes occasionally meeting Sudhakar's. She was poised, dressed in a simple yet elegant saree in a soft shade of blue, which complemented her calm demeanour. Her hair was neatly tied back, and she wore minimal jewellery—a pair of delicate earrings and a slender gold bracelet. There was something about her that immediately impressed Sudhakar, a combination of grace and intelligence that was unmistakable.

As the conversation flowed, Colonel Deshpande observed the interaction between Sudhakar and Radha. He could see the spark of interest in his daughter's eyes, and the way Sudhakar spoke with a blend of humility and confidence resonated with him. Sudhakar's practicality, his clear-headed approach to life, and, above all, his deep-seated patriotism, were qualities that Colonel Deshpande valued greatly. He had seen many young officers pass through the ranks, but there was something about

Sudhakar that stood out—a quiet determination and a sense of purpose that the Colonel admired.

By the end of the evening, Colonel Deshpande had made up his mind. He felt that Sudhakar would be an ideal companion for Radha. The Colonel believed that his daughter needed a partner who not only shared her values but also possessed the strength and stability that a life in the armed forces required. Sudhakar, with his unwavering dedication to his country and his pragmatic outlook on life, seemed to embody those very qualities.

As they bid each other goodnight, Colonel Deshpande placed a reassuring hand on Sudhakar's shoulder. "Take care, young man. I have a feeling we'll be seeing more of each other," he said with a knowing smile. Sudhakar, though unaware at the time, would come to realise the significance of those words in the months that followed.

That evening at the RSI Club was the beginning of a new journey, not just in Sudhakar's military career but in his personal life as well. The connection with Radha, sparked by that first meeting, would grow into a deep and abiding love, nurtured by the mutual respect and understanding that had been so evident in their initial interaction. And for Colonel Deshpande, seeing his daughter with a man like Sudhakar was the fulfilment of a hope that she would find someone who would cherish and support her as she deserved.

After two years of courtship filled with shared moments and growing affection, the time finally came for Sudhakar and Radha to formalise their bond. The families, having grown fond of each other over this period, met with mutual respect and understanding. The wedding was planned to be a small, intimate affair, reflecting the couple's preference for simplicity and meaning over grandeur.

The ceremony was held at the historic Bombay Sappers at Khadki, a place steeped in military tradition. The venue was symbolic, representing Sudhakar's deep connection to his military life and the shared values that had brought him and Radha together. The gathering was modest, consisting of Sudhakar's close family, a few of Radha's relatives, and his batch mates who had stood by him through thick and thin during their time at the NDA.

Radha looked radiant in a traditional silk saree, her gracefulness heightened by the simplicity of her attire. She wore minimal jewellery – a simple gold necklace, her mangalsutra, and a pair of earrings that had been a gift from her mother. Her hair was adorned with fresh jasmine flowers, their fragrance adding to the purity of the moment. Sudhakar, dressed in his formal military uniform, stood tall and composed, his presence commanding yet softened by the love he felt for Radha.

The very next day, with little time to spare, Sudhakar and Radha set off for Shillong. The North East awaited them, with its lush landscapes and the challenges that came with Sudhakar's posting. Life moved swiftly, and the couple soon found themselves immersed in their new surroundings, adapting to the rhythm of military life.

For Sudhakar, life was simple yet profoundly meaningful. He had two core priorities—his country and Radha. These were the twin pillars that supported his existence, giving him a purpose that was both clear and fulfilling. His love for Radha was intertwined with his sense of duty; they were not separate but complementary aspects of a life lived with honour and dedication. Radha, understanding this deep connection, supported him unconditionally, finding her own fulfilment in being by his side through the many challenges and adventures that lay ahead. Together, they formed a partnership that was not just about love but about shared values and a mutual commitment to living a life of purpose.

Sudhakar's mind wandered through the varied layers of his memories, each one a vivid snapshot of the life he and Radha had built together. The warmth of their wedding day, the shared laughter over countless dinners, the challenges they faced, and the quiet moments of companionship—all these recollections flowed through his mind, creating a comforting backdrop to the present.

But as his thoughts drifted back to reality, Sudhakar's attention shifted to Radha's current condition. Over the past couple of years, Radha had developed a routine that brought her great joy – a daily morning walk at 5:00 AM. Despite the society they lived in having a well-maintained walking track and a few friendly neighbours who also enjoyed morning strolls, Radha preferred to venture out of the gated community. She would walk around the corner outside the society, embracing the early morning tranquillity that the city offered at that hour.

This routine had become an essential part of her life, a time she cherished for its solitude and the peaceful connection it gave her with the world outside. Sudhakar knew that these walks brought her happiness. They allowed her to start her day with a sense of calm and purpose, providing a space where she could gather her thoughts and find inner peace.

He noticed that the walks made her calmer and more centred. The rhythm of her footsteps, the crisp morning air, and the gentle sounds of nature seemed to weave a soothing blanket over her thoughts, helping her greet each day with a clear mind and a peaceful heart. Sudhakar appreciated how much this routine meant to her, understanding that it was more than just exercise. It was a time for Radha to reconnect with herself, to find balance in the midst of life's demands.

Now, with Radha's current health condition, those walks were no longer possible. Sudhakar could see the toll it was taking on her. He felt a pang of sadness as he thought about how much she must miss those early mornings. The thought of her happiness being compromised troubled him deeply. The walks had been her sanctuary, a simple yet profound joy that now seemed so distant. This was yet another reminder of how much their lives had changed, and it fuelled Sudhakar's resolve to do everything in his power to support her recovery, hoping that, one day, she might be able to resume the routine that had brought her so much peace.

To Radha, the morning walk was more than just exercise; it was a mission, a purpose that filled a void in her life. One day, as she made her way to the corner of the street outside their society, she noticed a street dog. The sight of the dog, with its sad eyes and thin frame, sparked something within her – a deep sense of empathy. This feeling was a mix of her own loneliness, the ache of missing her children who had grown up and moved away, and the absence of the bustling energy of her days as a school teacher.

Driven by a desire to connect and perhaps to soothe some of her own heartache, Radha stopped at the kirana store just outside their society and bought a pack of Parle-G biscuits. She wasn't sure if the dog would eat them, but it was worth a try. As she approached the corner where she had seen the dog, she called out to him. The dog came trotting up to her with a cautious curiosity.

Radha opened the pack of biscuits, and before she could even count, the dog had devoured them all in a flash. His eagerness and the way he wagged his tail merrily, as if he had known her forever, warmed Radha's heart. An instant bond was born between them. What began as a simple act of feeding the dog with biscuits soon evolved into something more. Radha started bringing a bowl of milk and a few rotis for him, and she found herself looking forward to these encounters each morning.

The routine became a source of joy for her, a way to fill her days with purpose.

Sudhakar was aware of Radha's new routine and the joy it brought her. He didn't mind at all. In fact, he found comfort in knowing that she had found something that made her feel connected and needed. The dog had become a part of her life, a silent companion who brought a little extra happiness into her world. Radha's walks were no longer just about physical exercise; they were about love, compassion, and the simple joy of caring for another living being.

Over time, Radha's simple act of kindness blossomed into something much bigger. What started as a single dog eagerly devouring a pack of Parle-G biscuits slowly transformed into a growing community of street dogs. Each day, as Radha walked to her usual spot at the corner, another dog would join, then another. Before long, her morning routine involved not just one or two but fifteen dogs waiting for her arrival.

What had started as a small, spontaneous act of compassion had now become a significant part of Radha's life. She felt as though she had created a community, a small world where her care and attention were helping these street dogs survive in a harsh environment. The knowledge that her efforts were making a tangible difference in their lives gave her a profound sense of purpose. It was as if the loneliness she had once felt, the void left by her children's departure, and the absence of her teaching career had been filled by this new mission.

Radha's bond with the dogs deepened with each passing day. She learned their individual quirks, recognised their barks and even gave them names. The dogs, in turn, grew to trust her completely, sensing the kindness and love that radiated from her. They became her companions in a way, a source of comfort and joy that brightened her mornings.

For Radha, these morning walks had evolved far beyond a simple routine. They were a testament to the power of compassion, a reminder that even small acts of kindness could ripple outwards, creating a community and nurturing life. In feeding the dogs, she found herself nourished too, not just in body, but in spirit. She knew she had a purpose in all of this, and that knowledge gave her strength and peace, even as life continued to present its challenges.

Unfortunately, one fateful morning, as Radha was in the bathroom getting ready for her usual walk, the unthinkable happened. Her leg slipped, and she had a nasty fall. The sound of her body hitting the floor echoed through the quiet apartment, jolting Sudhakar awake. His heart raced as he rushed from his bed, calling out her name. When he reached her, he found Radha crumpled on the floor, her face twisted in agony. The pain was so intense that she couldn't move, and her voice trembled as she tried to speak.

Sudhakar felt a wave of panic, but knew he had to stay composed. He quickly called for an ambulance, and within minutes, they were rushing Radha to the hospital. Luckily, the Armed Forces Medical College (AFMC) hospital was nearby and well-equipped with advanced medical facilities. As a respected member of the defence fraternity, Sudhakar received immediate and comprehensive care for Radha, which brought him some measure of relief in the midst of his worry.

The doctors at AFMC diagnosed Radha with a severe hip fracture that required immediate surgery. Sudhakar stayed by her side, holding her hand and offering her words of comfort as she was wheeled into the operating room. His mind was a whirlwind of emotions: fear, concern, and a deep-seated hope that she would come through this ordeal safely.

Radha's surgery was successful – a hip replacement that would allow her to eventually regain her mobility. However, the recovery process was long and painful. Now back home, Radha was confined to bed, her movements restricted by the intense pain and the need to heal. The woman, who had once been so active and woke up before dawn each day to care for her beloved street dogs, was now bound to her bed, reliant on Sudhakar for everything.

As she lay there, Radha's thoughts often wandered to the corner of the society where she had fed the dogs without fail every morning. Little did she know what had happened there in her absence. She missed the routine, the joy of seeing the dogs wag their tails in anticipation, the sense of purpose it gave her each day. The dogs, too, must have been confused and hungry, waiting for the kind lady who had always been there for them, now suddenly gone without a trace.

Every morning, the scene at the corner of the society became increasingly unsettling. About fifteen street dogs would gather as they always had, but the peaceful routine Radha had established was now a distant memory. The dogs, once united by their mutual trust and affection for her, began to change. Without Radha's daily presence, their barking grew louder and more desperate, echoing through the tall buildings that surrounded them. It was as if they were crying out for her in unison, their voices merging into a haunting chorus of loss and confusion.

But the eerie harmony didn't last. After an hour of collective barking, the sound would shift to something far more ominous – the noise of dogs fighting. The once-peaceful pack had fragmented into warring factions, with dogs pouncing on each other in a primal struggle for dominance. The very corner that had been a place of care and connection had turned into a battleground. The dogs, now divided into groups, seemed to be locked in some kind of war, driven by instincts they had never needed to rely on before.

The call for Radha, which had initially been a cry of longing, gradually transformed into a call for survival. Without her to provide the ready-made food they had come to depend on, the dogs grew restless and aggressive. They had been conditioned to believe that food would always be readily available, that life would always be as simple as waiting for their morning meal. But now, faced with the need to fend for themselves, their inexperience led to chaos. Violence became their only means of coping with the world they suddenly found themselves in.

The situation grew worse with each passing day. The once-patient dogs turned on one another, driven by hunger and fear. The community Radha had nurtured was disintegrating, and the corner, once a place of compassion, became a site of brutality. The dogs' world had been turned upside down, and they had no understanding of why or how to navigate this new reality.

Then, one day, the inevitable happened. The municipal street dog van, responding to complaints from the neighbourhood, arrived at the corner. The sound of the dogs' barking and fighting had become too much for the residents, and the authorities decided to intervene. As the van pulled up, the dogs, unaware of what was to come, continued their frenzied struggle. The workers from the van, equipped with nets and cages, began rounding up the dogs one by one. The barking grew more frantic as the dogs were herded into the van, their fate sealed in a matter of minutes.

The van, now filled with the fifteen dogs, screeched away from the corner, leaving behind only silence. The dogs' cries, once a plea for Radha's return, now faded into the distance, their voices silenced by the harsh reality of their new circumstances. The fate of the dogs had been decided, not by their own actions, but by the circumstances thrust upon them – a harsh lesson in survival that came too late.

In the stillness that followed, a poignant truth lingered. Radha's care had been born out of kindness, but it had inadvertently sheltered the dogs from the realities of life. They had become dependent, unprepared for the world outside their routine. The once-loving act of feeding them had, over time, taken away their ability to fend for themselves.

This story is a stark reminder of the importance of teaching the art of survival—not just to our children, but to all who depend on us. There is no such thing as a free lunch; the world is a place where survival is earned through learning, facing challenges, and adapting to change. The dogs' story is a metaphor for life itself. Without the tools to survive, even the most caring environment can lead to unforeseen consequences.

As the van disappeared around the corner, the lesson was clear: survival is not just about sustenance. It's about resilience, adaptability, and the strength to face the world as it is, not just as we wish it to be.

Chapter 5

The Mentor

As the plane began its descent, Pands felt a flutter of anticipation in his chest. The vast blue of the sky gradually gave way to the sprawling cityscape of Mumbai, a city he had once known but had seen only in his memories for the past quarter-century. The flight had been long, but his mind had been restless, racing through memories of his childhood, his youth, and the life he had left behind.

When the wheels finally touched the tarmac, a tremor of emotion coursed through him. It wasn't just the relief of a safe landing; it was the profound realisation that he was back in the land that had shaped him. The scent of the air, even though the filtered cabin, carried a hint of something familiar—a mix of earthiness, warmth, and life. It was a scent he had never found anywhere else in the world.

As the plane taxied to the gate, Pands looked out of the window, his eyes drinking in the sight of trees swaying gently in the breeze, the distant outlines of buildings, and the hazy horizon. This was home. The word echoed in his mind, filling him with a sense of belonging he had almost forgotten.

The years abroad had been filled with achievements and opportunities, but they had also been marked by a subtle, persistent longing – a yearning for the place where his roots were anchored. No amount of success in foreign lands could replace the comfort of the familiar, the unspoken understanding that came from being among his own people, in his own culture.

As he prepared to disembark, his heart swelled with a mix of nostalgia and excitement. Every sound, every sight, every sensation felt magnified. He was eager to step off the plane, to feel the ground beneath his feet, to breathe in the humid air of Mumbai. It was more than just a return; it was a homecoming, a reconnection with a part of himself that had been waiting patiently, quietly, for this moment.

Pands knew that the India he was returning to was different from the one he had left behind. The country had changed, grown, and evolved, just as he had. But he also knew that some things would remain the same—the warmth of the people, the vibrancy of the culture, and the deep, unspoken bond he felt with the land. As he took his first steps back on Indian soil, Pands felt a surge of emotion that brought tears to his eyes. After twenty-five long years, he was home.

Pandurang, affectionately known as *Pands*, was a man of extraordinary intellect and unwavering determination. Born and raised in a modest family, he had always been fascinated by the mysteries of the universe. This fascination drove him to excel academically. His brilliance was evident from a young age, and by the time he completed his engineering degree in Pune, he had already made a name for himself as a student of exceptional promise.

Pands's journey to the United States was fuelled by his relentless pursuit of knowledge and his desire to push the boundaries of what was possible. The opportunity to study at MIT was a dream come true, made possible by a series of scholarships that recognised his academic prowess. At MIT, he was among the best and brightest from around the world, yet he stood out not just for his intellect, but for his dedication to his craft.

His work ethic and innovative thinking quickly caught the attention of his professors and peers alike. After completing his studies, Pands was offered a position at NASA, an opportunity he seized with both hands. His role now, as a lead aeronautics engineer, placed him at the forefront of some of the most ground-breaking projects in space exploration. He was instrumental in designing and developing complex systems for rockets, contributing to missions that expanded humanity's understanding of space.

In the United States, Pands built a life for himself that many would envy. He married a fellow engineer, and together, they raised two children who were now teenagers. His family was firmly rooted in American culture, thriving in the opportunities that the country offered. Pands, too, had grown accustomed to the fast-paced, innovation-driven environment of NASA, and his work had become a source of immense pride and satisfaction.

Yet, despite the accolades and the achievements, a part of Pands remained tethered to his roots. Over the years, the thought of returning to India had crossed his mind only fleetingly, quickly dismissed by the demands of his career and the life he had built in America. But as the years went by, something began to shift within him. The memories of his hometown, the streets he once walked, the familiar faces, and the cultural rhythms of his homeland began to occupy his thoughts more frequently.

The longing to reconnect with his roots grew stronger, a feeling that he found difficult to ignore. It was as if the call of his homeland was becoming more insistent, urging him to return, if only for a short while. It wasn't just nostalgia; it was a deep-seated need to reconnect to a part of himself that had been overshadowed by his life in the West.

The decision to make the trip was not easy. It meant stepping away from his responsibilities at work, even if temporarily, and leaving his family behind for a few weeks. But Pands knew that this journey was something he had to undertake. It was a journey of the heart, a pilgrimage back to the place that had given him his dreams and his identity. As he prepared for the trip, he couldn't help but wonder what awaited him in the land he had left behind so many years ago.

As Pands cleared customs, his heart pounded with excitement. He quickly grabbed his luggage, his eyes scanning the crowd for the driver. Amidst the early morning haze, he spotted a man holding a plaque that read:

"PANDS – NASA"

A small smile crept onto his face at the sight of his nickname paired with the prestigious organisation he had worked for over so many years. It felt surreal, seeing his identity from two different worlds converge in that simple sign.

It was 4:00 AM IST, and the air was cool and still, a sharp contrast to the hustle and bustle that would soon envelop the city as daylight broke. The driver, a middle-aged man with a kind but tired face, approached him, taking the luggage with practiced ease. Together, they made their way to the parking lot, the sound of their footsteps echoing softly in the quiet morning.

Pands felt a surge of anticipation as they reached the car. He was eager to get moving, to leave the confines of the airport and immerse himself in the familiar sights and sounds of India. As the car started, a wave of relief washed over him. They were on the move, and soon he would be on his way to the place that had been pulling at his heartstrings for years.

Mumbai, a city known for its relentless pace, had a different rhythm in the early hours of the morning. The roads, usually choked with traffic, were relatively clear, allowing the car to glide smoothly through the streets. Pands gazed out of the window, taking in the city as it stirred from its slumber. The buildings, the billboards, the occasional passer-by, they were all reminders that he was back, yet it all felt strangely new.

As the car weaved through Mumbai's towering skyline, Pands couldn't help but marvel at how the city had transformed. The once sprawling landscape had given way to gleaming skyscrapers that pierced the early morning sky, their glass façades reflecting the first light of dawn. The city had grown vertically, its ambitions as tall as the structures that now dominated the horizon. The sheer scale of development was awe-inspiring, yet it also felt distant from the simpler, quieter life he had once known.

As they reached the outskirts of the city, Pands leaned forward, his voice steady and filled with purpose. "Satara," he said to the driver, naming his destination. The driver nodded, and with a subtle press on the accelerator, the car picked up speed, heading toward the highway.

Satara. The name carried with it a flood of memories. It was more than just a town; it was the embodiment of his roots, the place where his dreams had been born. It was where his journey had begun, and now, after all these years, he was returning. The road stretched out before them, winding through the landscape that had once been so familiar. Pands settled into his seat, feeling the weight of the years fall away as they sped toward the heart of his past.

His thoughts drifted back to a time when the tallest structures he encountered were the trees that lined the fields of his village, Lonand, located close to Satara. It was a world far removed from the flashing billboards and towering buildings of Mumbai—a small, unassuming village near Satara, where the rhythm of life was dictated by the seasons and the sun.

As the car continued on its journey, a familiar voice echoed in his heart. A voice that had been his constant companion through the years.

"Remember, you have to believe in yourself, Panduranga. Dream. Dream big. Be audacious."

These were the words spoken to him by his mentor when he was a lad. They had been more than just advice; they were a mantra, a guiding light that had shaped his life.

At the time, those words seemed almost impossible to grasp. How could a boy from Lonand, a village so small it barely registered on a map, dream of anything more than the life that was laid out before him? But his mentor's words were insistent and they planted a seed of ambition in his young heart.

As he grew older, that seed began to take root. He studied hard, driven by the belief that his mentor had instilled in him. He dreamed of a life beyond the fields of Lonand, a life where he could reach for the stars—literally and figuratively. Those dreams carried him through the challenges of his education, through the gruelling hours of study and the pressure of exams. They pushed him to apply for scholarships, to take risks, and to leave behind everything he knew in pursuit of something greater.

And now, as he rode through the bustling streets of Mumbai, those dreams had brought him full circle. He had achieved more than he could have ever imagined, but the words that had guided him remained as true as ever. They were not just a call to action; they were a reminder of where he came from and how far he had travelled.

The city around him might have changed, grown, and evolved, but the essence of those dreams remained the same. And as his mind wandered back to Lonand, he felt a deep sense of gratitude for the journey that had brought him here. Soon, he would return to the place where it all began, the place where he first learned to dream.

Pandurang Ramchandra Karade, or Pands as he was affectionately known, had a life that was shaped by both hardship and determination. Born in the small, sleepy town of Lonand where life moved at its own unhurried pace, he was thrust into the harsh realities of life at a young age. Lonand, with its small population and simple way of life, was a place where dreams rarely extended beyond the borders of the town. But Pands was different. He had always felt a burning desire to rise above the circumstances that life had dealt him.

The loss of his parents when he was just 13 years old was a devastating blow, one that forced him to grow up quickly. With no siblings and only his father's sister to rely on, Pands had to navigate the challenges of life largely on his own. His aunt, though caring, could only do so much. The weight of responsibility fell squarely on his young shoulders, and he quickly learned that survival required hard work and resilience.

Despite the odds, Pands was determined to continue his education. Unlike many of the other children in the village who saw little use in schooling and were content with a life in the fields, Pands had a vision for something greater. He attended the local school, a modest institution with just a handful of students. The resources were scarce, the teachers were few, and the curriculum was limited, but Pands made the most of what he had. Every day, after school, he would head to the farms where he toiled under the hot sun to earn a small wage—just enough to keep himself fed.

The introduction to hardship at such an early age left a deep mark on Pands. He became introspective, often sitting alone, lost in thought. He wasn't just pondering the struggles of his daily life; he was searching for a way out, a path that would lead him to a better future. It was during these solitary moments that his determination to change his circumstances solidified. He refused to accept the status quo, and his mind became a crucible for big dreams and bold ambitions.

The turning point in Pands' life came after he completed his 10th standard. He had worked tirelessly, studying late into the night, determined to make a mark. Unlike the students in district towns who had access to coaching classes and other resources, Pands had to rely on his own grit and perseverance. But he was undeterred. He knew that education was his ticket to a different life, and he wasn't about to let anything stand in his way.

The success he achieved in his exams was more than just a personal victory; it was a beacon of hope. It confirmed what he had always believed—that with hard work and determination, he could overcome the limitations of his environment. This success was the first step on a long journey that would eventually take him far beyond the fields of Lonand, where his dreams would soar to unimaginable heights.

His memory jogged down to the time he finished his tenth exams. It was the final paper of history, a subject that always seemed to linger in the past, much like the memories Pands would later cherish. The relief of finishing the exams was palpable among the students, and Pands, who had been studying tirelessly for weeks, felt a mixture of exhaustion and exhilaration. During those intense 15 days of exams, he had formed a bond with a group of boys from Satara. They had spent their breaks discussing everything from their studies to their dreams, and now that the exams were over, there was a sense of finality in the air.

As they gathered outside the exam centre, the reality set in that this might be the last time they would all be together. The boys, eager to mark the occasion with something memorable, debated what to do next. At 17, their minds were filled with curiosity and a desire to explore the boundaries of adulthood. After much discussion, they decided to venture into a local bar, a place none of them had ever dared to enter before.

Pands, who had always been cautious and a bit reserved, hesitated. The excitement of his new friends was contagious, and he didn't want to be the odd one out. After all, this was a moment of camaraderie, a final hurrah before they all went their separate ways. He decided to go along with them, reasoning that there was no harm in sharing this experience, just once.

The bar was dimly lit, with a few scattered patrons who barely noticed the group of young boys as they nervously approached the counter. There was a thrill in the air, a mixture of fear and excitement, as they ordered a beer. Pands vividly remembers the name: Haywards 10000, a strong beer known for its potency. It was a bold choice, and the boys felt a surge of adrenaline as the words left their lips.

The waiter, a grizzled man who had likely seen his fair share of such rites of passage, eyed them sceptically. He asked twice to confirm the order, his eyes narrowing as he assessed whether these kids could pay. But the boys, filled with the bravado of youth, were resolute. With a nod, the waiter relented, fetching a bottle of Haywards 10000 along with five glasses and a plate of salted peanuts.

As he popped the cap off the bottle with a satisfying sound, the waiter couldn't help but grin. This was likely not the first time he had witnessed such a scene—teenage boys teetering on the edge of manhood, eager to take their first steps into the adult world. To him, it seemed almost like a divine duty to facilitate this transition, a role he embraced with a sense of pride. With a practiced hand, he poured the beer into the five glasses, filling each one equally. The boys watched in silence, their anticipation growing with each drop. When the glasses were finally full, the waiter handed them over with a look that seemed to say, "This is it, boys. Welcome to the next stage of your lives."

Pands took his glass, feeling its cool surface against his palm. He knew this was more than just a drink; it was a moment that would mark the end of one chapter and the beginning of another. As they raised their glasses in a silent toast, Pands couldn't help but feel a mix of emotions—nervousness and excitement. This was a moment he would carry with him for the rest of his life, a memory that would forever be associated with the bittersweet taste of that first sip of beer.

The anticipation was thick as all the lads looked at each other, waiting for someone to take the first daring step. The glasses filled with chilled beer glistened under the dim lights of the bar, almost daring them to cross the threshold from boyhood to something more. Pands, feeling the weight of their expectant gazes, picked up his glass. With a mix of determination and trepidation, he brought it to his lips and took a large gulp.

The sensation was immediate and intense – a fiery trail burned down his throat, hitting his stomach with a force that sent a shockwave through his entire body. His head buzzed with a strange, electrifying current, and for a brief moment, he was disoriented, trying to process what had just happened. As he blinked and looked up, he saw his friends staring at him in shock, their hands still clutching their untouched glasses.

The moment hung in the air until, as if on cue, the other boys found their own courage. Inspired by Pands' boldness, they each raised their glasses and followed his lead, downing their beers in one go. What followed was a blur of gibberish and laughter, the kind of wild, uninhibited merriment that only comes from breaking the rules for the first time. The waiter, watching from a distance, smiled to himself, feeling like he had just won some unspoken game. He had seen it all before—the wide-eyed innocence, the reckless bravado, the inevitable descent into tipsy exuberance.

One beer led to another, and before they knew it, they had polished off five bottles between the five of them. For a group of first-timers, this was nothing short of a feat, one that even the seasoned waiter found impressive. By 8:00 PM, the boys were well past the point of sobriety, their minds swimming in the unfamiliar warmth of alcohol. The world outside the bar faded into insignificance as they revelled in their newfound freedom.

But reality eventually caught up with them. The other boys, realising the time, hurried off, their steps unsteady as they rushed home to avoid the wrath of worried parents. Pands, on the other hand, had to catch the last bus back to Lonand at 11:00 PM. His memories of that part of the night were hazy at best. He vaguely recalled stumbling out of the bar, the cool night air hitting him like a splash of cold water. The next thing he knew, he was being shaken awake by the bus conductor, who was urgently trying to wake him up.

"Lonand! Your stop, kid!" the conductor barked, his voice cutting through the fog in Pands' head.

Groggily, Pands stumbled off the bus, his legs unsteady beneath him. He had no recollection of how he had managed to board the bus or how he had found his seat. All he knew was that he had somehow made it back to Lonand, his head spinning with the events of the night. As he stood on the familiar dusty road, the memories of the evening slowly began to settle, leaving him with a strange mix of pride, embarrassment, and the faintest tinge of regret. It had been a night of firsts.

It was fifteen minutes past 1:00 AM, and the village lay still under the soft glow of moonlight, with shadows dancing across the dirt paths that Pands treaded. His steps were light, almost as if he were floating, still under the influence of the evening's indulgence. The beer had left him in a strange, dreamlike state, where every thought felt profound, every sensation heightened. His head was buzzing with random ideas, and he found himself humming a tune, a rhythm in his steps that seemed to propel him forward without effort.

The night was cool, and the air was thick with the scent of earth and foliage. As Pands neared the edge of the village, the silhouette of the ancient banyan tree came into view. It was a massive, imposing presence, its sprawling roots and thick branches having stood as silent witnesses to the stories of countless generations. The tree had always been there, a steadfast guardian of the village, and as Pands approached, he couldn't help but feel a strange sense of reverence.

Just as he was about to pass the tree, a voice called out,

"Panduranga, Panduranga..."

The voice was soft, almost familiar, and it sent a shiver down his spine. It had the tone and cadence similar to his father's voice, a sound that he hadn't heard in years. He stopped in his tracks, his heart pounding, as he looked around, trying to find the source of the voice. But there was no one in sight, only the moonlight that bathed the landscape in a silver glow, casting long shadows across the ground.

He looked up at the tree, its branches swaying gently in the breeze. Was it the beer playing tricks on his mind? Was he imagining things? He shook his head, trying to clear his thoughts, but the sense of unease lingered. Then, without warning, he felt a cold hand on his shoulder, sending a jolt of fear through his entire body. He spun around, his breath caught in his throat.

Standing before him was a young man, no older than twenty, with an appearance that was as unsettling as it was strange. His clothes were outdated, like something from a bygone era, and his skin was pale, almost ghostly. But it was his eyes that captured Pands' attention—eyes that sparkled with an unnatural light, in stark contrast to his otherwise spectral demeanour. The man was lanky, his figure almost fragile, and yet there was something about him that felt otherworldly, as if he didn't quite belong to the world of the living.

Pands stared at the stranger, his mind racing to make sense of what he was seeing. The man's presence was both eerie and intriguing, as if he was caught between two realms, neither fully alive nor fully dead. The young man's gaze was intense, holding Pands in place as if searching for something deep within him.

The silence stretched between them, thick and heavy, until the young man finally spoke. His voice was low and resonant, "You've come a long way, Panduranga, but the journey isn't over yet." His words hung in the air, filled with a meaning that Pands couldn't quite grasp, yet they stirred something deep within him – an ancient, primal fear mixed with a strange sense of destiny.

Pands didn't know what to say; his voice caught in his throat as he tried to respond. But before he could utter a word, the young man's grip on his shoulder tightened for just a moment, then released. The stranger took a step back, his form beginning to fade into the shadows of the banyan tree, as if he were being absorbed back into the darkness from which he had emerged.

"Remember, Panduranga," the voice echoed one last time, softer now, almost a whisper, "Dream big. Be audacious."

And then, just as suddenly as he had appeared, the young man was gone, leaving Pands alone under the banyan tree, the night air still and silent once more. Pands stood there, shaken and bewildered, his mind reeling from the encounter. Was it a figment of his imagination, a hallucination brought on by the alcohol, or was there something more, something deeper, and more mysterious at play?

As he resumed his walk towards home, the words of the stranger lingered in his mind, intertwining with the memories of his father, the ancient tree, and the life he had. The journey ahead seemed more uncertain than ever, but one thing was clear—something had shifted within him, something that would stay with him for the rest of his days.

Under the ancient banyan tree, where the moonlight cast ethereal shadows, Pands met *Gopal*, a figure who seemed both familiar and otherworldly. Gopal's introduction was simple yet profound, "I am Gopal.". There was something about his presence that intrigued Pands, something he couldn't quite put his finger on. Gopal's calm demeanour and the strange comfort he brought felt like a lifeline to Pands, who had never had a father figure or anyone to guide him through the complexities of life.

"Don't be scared, Panduranga," Gopal said, his voice soothing. "I'm here to speak to you. You see, I was born in this village, and I've been watching you work so hard. I thought it would be great to share my life lessons with you. I believe they might help you."

Pands felt a warmth in Gopal's presence, a sense of reassurance that he had long been searching for. Every night, the two of them sat down beneath the sprawling branches of the banyan tree, and Gopal would talk. His words flowed like a river, full of wisdom and insights that resonated deeply with Pands. It felt as if he was sitting before a guru, someone who was unravelling the mysteries of life and handing him the keys to a greater understanding.

The time melted away every night as Gopal spoke, sharing stories from his own life. Each tale was a lesson in itself. He talked about the importance of dreaming big, the challenges of dealing with people, and the subtle ways society tries to pull you down. Pands listened intently, absorbing every word as if it were a sacred teaching.

Pands made it a habit to visit the banyan tree to meet Gopal. Each night, under the cover of darkness, they would sit together, and Gopal would continue to share his life lessons. The topics were wide-ranging, from understanding people's behaviour to nurturing big dreams, and every conversation left Pands feeling more enlightened and empowered.

For almost a month, these nocturnal meetings became a ritual. Pands would often find himself waking up under the banyan tree, not tired, but rather rejuvenated, with a deeper awareness of life's complexities and a stronger resolve to pursue his dreams. The banyan tree became a place of learning where Pands' mind was sharpened, and his spirit lifted by the mysterious teachings of Gopal.

On this clear, full moon night, Pands arrived at the banyan tree well before his usual time. The moonlight bathed the village in a serene glow, casting long, silvery shadows across the ground. As Pands approached the familiar spot, he noticed a figure already seated beneath the tree. It was Gopal, but tonight there was an unmistakable sadness in his eyes that Pands had never seen before.

Gopal's usual demeanour was replaced with a quiet solemnity as he placed a hand gently on Pands' shoulder. His voice, though soft, carried a weight of profound emotion.

"You see, Panduranga," Gopal began, "life is very simple. It is very beautiful. We humans make it complicated. Our lives are full of expectations. The moment you shift your expectations from other people to expecting from yourself, you are on a path to change yourself. The journey of self-actualisation and self-improvement begins at that point."

Pands listened intently, his own feelings of unease mirrored by the sombre tone in Gopal's words. There was something deeply moving about Gopal's expression, something that hinted at a personal struggle or realisation.

"Happiness," Gopal continued, "is not something others will give you; it is what you give to others. It could be as simple as sharing your learnings and life lessons, just like I am doing now. It gives me a tremendous sense of completion and happiness, Panduranga."

The weight of Gopal's words sank in. There was a profound sincerity in what he was saying, a sense of fulfilment that came from contributing to someone else's growth. Gopal's own purpose seemed deeply entwined with guiding Pands, and this revelation added layers to his character that Pands had not fully understood before.

"If I am able to inspire one person and put him on the right path," Gopal said, his voice carrying a sense of peace. "I have served my life's purpose. I want you to dream. Dream big, dream audacious. Work every ounce of your energy and time to achieve what you have set out for. You will dream, and you will achieve. Nobody but you, are the only one who will help yourself reach your goal."

Gopal's gaze was unwavering, his words filled with conviction. "The society will pull you down. They will laugh at you, they will kill your confidence. Let them do what they feel is right. You choose your battlefield and your wins. Life is that simple."

As the moonlight danced through the leaves, Gopal's message was clear and resonant. He spoke of personal responsibility, the power of self-belief, and the simplicity of life when stripped of external expectations. The sadness in his eyes seemed to reflect a deeper truth, one that he had come to terms with through his own experiences.

Pands sat in silence, absorbing the gravity of Gopal's teachings. The sadness in Gopal's eyes now felt like a mirror, reflecting the struggles and complexities of his own journey. Yet, there was also a profound clarity in Gopal's words, a beacon guiding him through the fog of uncertainty.

As they sat together beneath the banyan tree, the full moon casting its serene light over them, Pands felt a renewed sense of purpose. Gopal's lessons were more than just guidance; they were a gift, a legacy of wisdom that Pands would carry with him. The path ahead seemed clearer, the battles more defined, and the dreams within reach. With Gopal's words echoing in his mind, Pands was ready to embrace the simplicity of life, to dream boldly, and to pursue his goals with unwavering determination.

"You know, Panduranga," Gopal said softly, his voice carrying a note of finality. "Today is the last time we are meeting. My mission is done. I think I have completed the job after 50 years. My soul is now free to go!"

The gravity of Gopal's statement hit Pands with full force. The realisation that this was their final meeting brought a surge of sorrow and gratitude. Tears welled up in Pands' eyes, and despite his effort to hold them back, they began to roll down his cheeks.

Gopal's gaze was kind, filled with a mix of sadness and satisfaction. "Remember my words and be good. Make sure you inspire one person along your journey and give him/her a reason to live, and live meaningfully."

Before Pands could respond, Gopal's form began to dissolve into a cascade of shimmering light particles. The transformation was both beautiful and haunting, as if Gopal was becoming one with the very essence of the moonlit night. The light grew brighter, enveloping him, until Gopal was no longer there—just a fleeting memory and a lingering glow.

Pands sat alone beneath the banyan tree, the emptiness of Gopal's absence heavy in the air. The moonlight seemed to take on a more profound significance, casting an almost ethereal glow over the spot where Gopal had vanished. The lessons, the inspiration, and the wisdom imparted were now a part of Pands, etched deeply into his soul.

As the night wore on, Pands remained seated, reflecting on the powerful words and the emotional farewell. The experience was both a closure and a beginning, a poignant end to a chapter of guidance and the start of a new journey marked by Gopal's teachings.

The banyan tree stood silent, a witness to the meeting and the departure. Pands felt a renewed sense of purpose and commitment to live by Gopal's words – to dream big, to strive for his goals, and to pass on the inspiration to others. With a heavy heart but a determined spirit, he prepared to continue his journey, carrying with him the light of Gopal's wisdom and the promise to inspire others just as he had been inspired.

As the car came to a stop at the banyan tree, Pands felt a rush of deep emotion, similar to what he had experienced during his last encounter with Gopal. The tree stood as a symbol of both remembrance and inspiration. Pands had travelled all the way from the USA to honour Gopal's memory and to inaugurate the local school he had funded and helped establish.

Standing there, Pands felt a profound sense of accomplishment. The school was a testament to Gopal's legacy and Pands' commitment to making a difference. It was more than just a building; it represented the dreams and hopes of countless children who would have access to education and the chance to aspire beyond their immediate circumstances.

Gopal's tragic story came full circle in Pands' mind. At just 20, Gopal had been killed by rowdy locals who felt betrayed by his departure from the village to pursue a career in acting. His dreams, which had seemed so distant and audacious at the time, had cost him his life. Yet, Gopal's spirit, once troubled by the unfulfilled potential, had found solace in knowing that his teachings had inspired Pands. The light Gopal had seeded had indeed germinated, reaching new minds and encouraging them to dream boldly.

Standing by the banyan tree, Pands felt a deep connection to Gopal's memory. The tree, once a silent witness to their conversations, now symbolised the enduring impact of Gopal's wisdom. The local school, with its promise of education and opportunity, was a tribute to the spirit of dreaming big and making a difference.

As he paid his silent homage, Pands was filled with gratitude and resolve. The journey from Lonand to NASA had come full circle, and now, with the school's inauguration, Pands felt a sense of completion. His mission was aligned with Gopal's vision: to inspire, to dream, and to make a meaningful impact on the world.

Chapter 6

Mr. Kulkarni

He looked at himself in the mirror of the office washroom. A man on the doorstep of his retirement. Balding, with a short stature and a protruding belly. Slightly bent, perhaps from the worries of life. His large glasses covered one third of his bulky face.

As he combed the remainder of his hair, a sigh of relief escaped his lips. With a renewed vigour to start his day and leave his worries behind, Mr. Kulkarni stepped out of the washroom and began his day. Mr. Kulkarni had been working with the company located in the heart of Pune, Erandwane, for the last 30 years. He was part of the accounts team, managing day-to-day accounting and paperwork. Although very meticulous with his work, he never aspired to climb the ranks throughout his career. Despite being well-suited for higher positions, he always let opportunities pass him by.

He was the first person to reach the office every day and the first to leave, always punctual. A man of few words and dedicated to his work, he appeared to lack social skills and had little inclination to make friends. Observing his demeanour, one could easily conclude that he had few, if any, friends.

"Are you new to the company? What is this?" yelled Mr. Kulkarni, his voice echoing through the office. Sudhakar, the new joiner, felt his heart pound as he faced the veteran's wrath. This was his first job, and in his first month, he had already made a blunder. Mr. Kulkarni was known for his sharp tongue and unwavering insistence on following procedures to the letter. Today, Sudhakar had submitted his travel claim for reimbursement but had neglected to attach the receipts. That seemingly minor oversight had triggered Mr. Kulkarni's outburst.

The entire office fell silent, the tension palpable. Sudhakar felt everyone's eyes on him, making his face flush with embarrassment. He could barely meet Mr. Kulkarni's gaze, which was piercing and unforgiving.

"Sorry, Sir. I didn't realise..." Sudhakar stammered, his voice barely audible.

"Didn't realise? This is basic! If you can't handle simple tasks, how do you expect to manage more significant responsibilities?" Mr. Kulkarni snapped, cutting him off. "Make sure this doesn't happen again."

The incident left Sudhakar not just disturbed, but deeply shaken. He replayed the scene in his mind, wondering how he had missed such a crucial detail. Could Mr. Kulkarni have told him in a better way? Was this how he treated everyone, or was it just the fate of new employees?

From that day on, Sudhakar kept a close eye on Mr. Kulkarni. He became almost obsessed with understanding the man behind the stern exterior. Was he the same person at home, strict and demanding? What about his family? Did they also walk on eggshells around him?

Sudhakar imagined Mr. Kulkarni's household – a place ruled with the same iron fist he wielded at work. Did his wife and children fear him, or was there a softer side to the man that his colleagues never saw?

As days turned into weeks, Sudhakar observed Mr. Kulkarni's every move. He noticed how Mr. Kulkarni was always the first to arrive at the office, meticulously organising his workspace before anyone else walked in. He was the first to leave as well, precisely on time, as if he had a schedule down to the minute. His dedication was unquestionable, but his interactions were always curt, almost devoid of warmth.

Sudhakar's curiosity grew. He wondered if there was a hidden story behind Mr. Kulkarni's stern demeanour. Perhaps he had faced hardships that had hardened him, or maybe he simply believed that discipline was the key to success. Whatever the reason, Sudhakar couldn't shake off the feeling that there was more to Mr. Kulkarni than met the eye.

The incident became a turning point for Sudhakar. It drove him to excel, to ensure he never gave Mr. Kulkarni a reason to scold him again. But it also sparked a determination to unravel the mystery of the man who had become a figure of both fear and fascination in his life.

One day, Sudhakar decided to finally follow Mr. Kulkarni after work. His curiosity had been eating away at him, and he needed to understand the man beyond the stern facade. Ensuring that Mr. Kulkarni didn't notice him, Sudhakar kept a safe distance.

That particular day, Mr. Kulkarni hurriedly walked out of the office gate, not even glancing at the security guards, as if he was on an important mission. He took a left turn and crossed the street, stopping at a popular vada paav stall called 'Manik Vada Paav'. The stall, which opened at 4:30 PM, was already gathering a crowd. Known for its spicy and irresistible vada paavs, it was a favourite among the local office workers.

Mr Kulkarni quickly parcelled four vada paavs. Sudhakar, watching from a distance, wondered why Mr Kulkarni didn't eat there and why he bought four vada paavs. Puzzled, he continued to follow as Mr Kulkarni paid and moved swiftly towards his house.

After a 300-metre walk, Mr Kulkarni stopped at a small gate leading to a bungalow. He unlocked it and entered. Sudhakar observed the bungalow, a modest one with trees and a garden, but with faded paint that hinted at past glory and current neglect.

Mr Kulkarni hurried from the veranda and opened the main door with his keys. Sudhakar stayed hidden, watching intently. Five minutes passed. Mr Kulkarni emerged with a coffee table, followed by two chairs, setting them up neatly before going inside again. This time, he brought out the vada paavs on plates along with tea—two plates, two cups. Sudhakar's curiosity peaked.

Mr Kulkarni went inside once more and came out after five minutes, this time pushing a wheelchair. Seated in the wheelchair was a woman, presumably his wife, who appeared to be around the same age. Sudhakar's heart sank when he realised she was paralysed, her body motionless except for a content smile resting on one side of her face. She looked genuinely happy with Mr Kulkarni by her side.

Sudhakar's eyes welled up with tears as he understood the pain behind Mr. Kulkarni's stern demeanour. He turned and walked away, heading back to his own home. He couldn't shake off the profound sadness he felt, reflecting on his own loneliness and the hidden side of Mr. Kulkarni.

Mr Kulkarni's children had left for the USA 17 years ago to pursue higher education and settled there. After getting married, they never returned. Eight years ago, his wife had suffered a paralysis attack. Since then, Mr Kulkarni had devoted himself entirely to her care. His life revolved around her needs and happiness, and all the struggles and achievements of his life seemed to be fading away.

Everyone carries hidden burdens and untold stories that shape their behaviour and actions. Before judging others, it's essential to understand their circumstances and the silent battles they might be fighting. Compassion, empathy, and understanding can reveal the true depth of a person's character and the sacrifices they make for the ones they love.

Sudhakar walked away from Mr. Kulkarni's gate, no longer needing any further explanation. He now understood the weight Mr. Kulkarni carried and the depth of his silent sacrifice.

Chapter 7

Retirement

━━━━━◆◆━━━━━

Beep!

Beep!!

Beep!!!

The constant beeps of the electrocardiogram pierced deeply into Sudha's heart as she sat beside her husband's ICU bed in the hospital.

Unaware of the tension gripping his wife, Sudha, he remained in a state of unconsciousness, detached from the worry and fear consuming her. Sudha sat vigilantly by his side, her eyes filled with tears that she fought to hold back. The constant beeps of the electrocardiogram felt like daggers piercing her heart, each one a reminder of the fragility of her husband's life.

At 65, Gajendra Gangadhar Patil weighed a mere 50 kilograms, his once robust frame now emaciated and frail. He had almost entirely lost his muscular mass, leaving behind a body that was a shadow of its former self. His skin clung tightly to his bones, his eyes bulging out from their sockets, and his cheeks hollowed. His rib cage was starkly visible through the thin fabric of his hospital gown, rising and falling with each laboured breath.

The marks from syringes on his wrists were stark and numerous, proof of the difficulty the medical staff had in finding his veins. Each puncture wound was a small battle scar in his fight for survival, showcasing the relentless efforts to keep him alive. His hands lay limp by his sides, the IV tubes delivering a lifeline of medicine and blood into his veins.

The room was filled with the scent of antiseptic and the low hum of the various machines keeping Gajendra alive. The saline tubes attached to him were like lifelines, one pouring blood, and the other medicine into his body. Each drop matched the pacing heartbeat of Sudha, who clung to hope despite the overwhelming odds. Her mind raced with memories of better times and the fear of an uncertain future.

Sudha's heart ached as she watched her husband's still form. The weight of the situation pressed down on her, making it hard to breathe. Every beep, every laboured breath, every drop of medicine, was a reminder of the precarious balance between life and death. She reached out and gently held her husband's hand, willing her strength into him, hoping for a miracle that would bring him back to her.

Her past life sprinted before her eyes, and she questioned herself as to why her once happy life had taken a fateful turn to this juncture.

Gaja, fondly called, was born in Saswad, 45 km from Pune, to a farming family. He was a man whose presence was impossible to ignore. From a young age, his physique seemed to be cautiously chiselled by God, each muscle and sinew a testament to his strength and vitality. By the time he reached 20, Gaja stood at an imposing 6 feet 3 inches, his well-built frame exuding power and confidence. His sharp eyes could tear through anyone who dared to cross his path, a reflection of his unwavering determination and inner strength.

Growing up, Gaja had a deep love for Kushti, the traditional Indian form of wrestling. His passion for the sport shaped his daily routine, which included rigorous exercises and a disciplined lifestyle. He would rise before dawn, his day beginning with a series of demanding physical workouts designed to enhance his strength, agility, and endurance. His regimen included everything from lifting heavy weights to practicing intricate wrestling techniques, all performed with a level of dedication that set him apart from his peers.

Gaja's diet was equally impressive, a necessity given his demanding exercise routine. He consumed large quantities of wholesome, nutritious food, a diet that would put anyone to shame with its sheer volume. Fresh milk, ghee, almonds, and a variety of vegetables and meats made up his meals, fuelling his body for the gruelling training sessions and the physically demanding matches he participated in.

His presence was formidable; the weight of his physical demeanour could petrify any ordinary person. When Gaja entered a room, conversations would halt, and all eyes would turn towards him. There was a raw, primal energy about him, a silent assertion of dominance that needed no words. People respected him, not just for his physical prowess, but also for the discipline and commitment that radiated from him.

Despite his intimidating exterior, those who knew Gaja well understood that beneath his rugged surface lay a heart full of warmth and kindness. He was fiercely loyal to his family and friends, always ready to lend a hand or stand up for those in need. His strong moral compass and sense of justice were as pronounced as his physical strength, making him a revered figure in his community.

Gaja had a successful career in wrestling at both local and national levels during his younger days. His exceptional skills and dedication to the sport earned him numerous accolades, making him a well-known figure in the wrestling community. His father was particularly proud of Gaja's achievements and held high hopes for his future, dreaming of a well-educated bride for his accomplished son.

Gaja's father's wishes came true when Gaja married Sudha. The couple appeared to be a match made in heaven, complementing each other perfectly. Sudha was not only well-educated but also shared Gaja's values of hard work and dedication. Together, they made an impressive and harmonious pair.

Leveraging his wrestling success, Gaja secured a government job through the sports quota. His life seemed to be the epitome of perfection. For six years, he worked diligently in Pune, where their first child was born. The arrival of their baby brought immense joy to the couple, further solidifying their bond. Gaja and Sudha embraced their new roles as parents with enthusiasm and love.

Following Gaja's transfer, the family moved to Mumbai where they welcomed their second child. Despite the challenges that came with relocating and adjusting to a new city, Gaja managed his official duties and family responsibilities with remarkable ease. He found a fine balance between his work and personal life, ensuring that neither was neglected.

In Mumbai, Gaja's commitment to his job and family remained steadfast. He excelled in his professional role while being an attentive and loving husband and father. His ability to juggle multiple responsibilities made him a role model for many. Sudha and Gaja, in particular, were content with how their children were growing up, witnessing their kids thrive in a nurturing and supportive environment.

The family's life was filled with moments of happiness and contentment. Weekends were often spent together, exploring the vibrant city of Mumbai or enjoying quiet family time at home. Gaja's presence was a source of strength and stability for Sudha and the children. He instilled values of discipline, hard work, and integrity in his kids, just as he had been taught by his own father.

Now, as Sudha sat by Gaja's hospital bed, the memories of their beautiful journey together flooded her mind. She remembered the strong, resilient man who had been her partner through all of life's ups and downs. The contrast between the robust wrestler who once dominated the arena and the fragile figure lying before her was heart-wrenching. Yet, amidst the beeping machines and the sterile hospital environment, she held on to the hope that Gaja's indomitable spirit would once again triumph, just as it had so many times before.

Gaja worked with the government all his life and retired at fifty-eight. His retirement ceremony was particularly noteworthy as many of his colleagues recounted the ethics and vigour with which Gaja had surpassed many challenging projects and assignments. He treated his work as the next game he wanted to win. Sudha and their children were especially proud of him, particularly when his colleagues and previous bosses spoke highly of his dedication and integrity.

Post-retirement, his energy levels remained high despite his ageing body. With their children now married and living separately, it was just Sudha and Gaja left to their own company. Gaja maintained a rigorous routine, going for a jog every morning at 5 AM and every evening at 5 PM. However, despite his regular exercise, he began to look pale and tired after his walks. Sudha grew increasingly worried as his daily food intake diminished. Over the next four years, Gaja's health steadily declined, leaving doctors puzzled about his condition. Sudha spent these years in constant worry, urging Gaja to see a doctor, but he resisted.

Two days ago, Gaja returned from his walk and sat down on a stool to remove his shoes. Suddenly, there was a loud thud as he collapsed from the chair. Sudha, hearing the noise, rushed in from the kitchen to find Gaja unconscious on the floor. She called for help, and their neighbours quickly arrived, rushing Gaja to the hospital where he was immediately taken to the intensive care unit. Fortunately, he survived the incident.

Sudha spent the entire night by Gaja's side, holding his hand and praying fervently. In the early hours of the morning, Gaja's hand moved, waking Sudha. She opened her eyes to see Gaja's deep-set eyes looking back at her. In a faint voice, he murmured, "Sudha, don't tell the kids."

Sudha cursed herself for what had eventually happened. A week before, out of suspicion, she had followed him on his morning walk. Gaja walked two kilometres from their house to an old tree from where they lived. There, he would pick up a hidden bottle of rum, 250 ml, and drink it quickly. Sudha couldn't believe her eyes. Gaja had been following this routine since his retirement, and eventually, his body had taken a toll.

"Promise me, you will stop it, and I will not tell the kids," Sudha said, her voice firm but loving.

Sudha knew that the man lying in the hospital bed possessed immense willpower and believed he would overcome this. At that moment, she did not want to think about what had prompted Gaja to start drinking. Instead, she looked forward to spending the remainder of their time together peacefully and healthily.

Even the strongest among us can fall prey to hidden struggles. It's essential to address issues openly and support each other through tough times. True strength lies not just in physical prowess, but in facing one's vulnerabilities and seeking help when needed. Sudha's unconditional support and Gaja's willingness to change highlighted the power of love, understanding, and the human spirit's resilience.

Chapter 8

Candle Light Dinner

The rope hung outside the door, innocuously inviting any visitor to announce their arrival with a simple tug. Its weathered appearance belied the peculiar charm of the man behind the door, Abhay Patwardhan, affectionately known as Pitya. To those unfamiliar, the board's directive to *"Pull the rope to ring a bell"* seemed straightforward enough, yet it concealed an element of surprise that Sammy, on his first visit, was soon to discover.

Sammy approached the door with a mix of anticipation and curiosity. He had heard tales of Pitya's eccentricities – his daring escapades, his deep-rooted love for animals, and his penchant for the unusual. As he reached out and grasped the rope, a sudden screech shattered the quietude, sending a shiver down Sammy's spine. Startled, he hesitated for a moment, uncertain of what had just transpired. Summoning his courage, he pulled the rope again, only to be greeted by an even louder screech, this time unmistakably that of a bat.

Before Sammy could ponder the strange occurrences any further, the door swung open with a swift creak. There stood Pitya, his presence commanding yet strangely inviting, a smile playing on his lips as if he anticipated Sammy's reaction all along.

"Welcome to the world of Pitya," he announced with a hint of mischief in his voice, beckoning Sammy into a realm that defied conventional norms and embraced the unconventional with open arms.

The interior of Pitya's home was a testament to his singular character – a blend of rustic charm and wild eccentricities. Posters adorned the walls, each depicting a different species of snakes from around the world, their vibrant colours and intricate patterns capturing the essence of Pitya's fascination with reptilian creatures. In one corner, a collection of feathers in every hue imaginable adorned the space, a testament to his admiration for avian beauty and diversity.

Sammy, overwhelmed by the sensory feast before him, felt as though he had stepped into a jungle sanctuary rather than an urban apartment. Pitya, noticing his guest's wide-eyed wonder, moved effortlessly through the room, his demeanour a mix of gentle hospitality and unapologetic quirkiness.

He handed Sammy a steaming cup of donkey's milk, its contents thick and rich. Sammy hesitated briefly, unsure of what to expect, but the genuine enthusiasm in Pitya's eyes encouraged him to take a sip. The milk, surprisingly pleasant, carried a hint of earthiness that lingered on his palate, a testament to Pitya's eclectic tastes and unwavering.

As Sammy savoured the unusual beverage, his gaze wandered to a curious sight – a crow perched near the window, its right wing carefully splinted and supported. The unexpected sight prompted Sammy to inquire, his curiosity piqued by the scene before him.

"Pitya, what happened to the crow?" Sammy ventured, his voice filled with both awe and curiosity. Pitya's expression softened, a flicker of empathy crossing his features, as he regarded the injured bird with affectionate concern.

"Ah, him," Pitya replied, his voice tinged with a mixture of compassion and admiration. "Found him just last night, injured and alone. Brought him here, tended to his wing. He'll be flying again soon."

Sammy listened, captivated by Pitya's dedication to the creatures he so clearly adored. It was a sentiment that ran deeper than mere fascination; it was a profound respect for life in all its forms, a belief in the inherent value of every living being.

Pitya, a character very unique and charmingly creepy. Daring to take on any challenge, his stories of daring were out of this world. One such challenge he accepted was to ride his bike at 5 am in winter on Law College Road, bare-clothed! He passed with flying colours without breaking a sweat.

Pitya's audacious exploits were legendary, each tale contributing to the mythos surrounding his enigmatic persona. The stories of his bold endeavours could fill volumes, but one night would never suffice to recount them all. During his college days, Pitya developed a distinctive habit that set him apart from his peers: chewing tobacco. Among his group of friends, he was the sole adherent to this vice, but it was not merely the act itself that intrigued others—it was his meticulous approach.

Pitya was exceptionally particular about his brand of tobacco and the ritualistic manner in which he consumed it. From a leather pouch marked with his initials, he would draw the exact amount of tobacco needed. The pouch seemed almost like an extension of Pitya himself. His method was precise: five minutes of thorough rubbing with his right thumb on his left palm, no more, no less. Observing Pitya engaged in this process was akin to witnessing an artist at work, the rhythmic motions hypnotic in their consistency and dedication.

Once the tobacco was properly prepared, Pitya would produce a small round steel box containing 'chuna', or lime. With a flick of his wrist that could rival the agility of a martial artist, he would deftly extract a small quantity of chuna and mix it with the tobacco. The mixture was then passed from hand to hand, ensuring even distribution and removing any impurities. Finally, with the precision of a craftsman, he would place the prepared tobacco in the right corner of his mouth, snug between his lips and teeth.

This ritual, repeated with unwavering consistency, was a spectacle for those who watched. For about thirty minutes, the tobacco would sit there, releasing its juices, which Pitya would either suck or spit out. His spits were precise, landing on the exact spot every time, a testament to the practiced perfection of his habit. The brand remained the same, the ritual unchanged, and so did Pitya—a man steadfast in his ways, embodying a peculiar blend of tradition and eccentricity.

"Why are you like this, Pitya?" Sammy finally asked, unable to contain his curiosity any longer. "Your love for animals, your daring escapades—it's all so unconventional," he added.

Pitya regarded Sammy with a knowing smile, his eyes reflecting years of experience and a deep-seated philosophy that guided his every action.

"Sammy, animals—they are pure," Pitya explained, his voice resonant with conviction. "They ask for nothing but offer everything. In their presence, I find solace, companionship, and a profound sense of belonging. Humans, on the other hand, complicate simplicity, often taking more than they give."

He paused, a wistful expression briefly clouding his features, before he continued.

"I choose to live authentically, to embrace the wonders of nature, and protect those who cannot protect themselves. It is a calling, a path I have chosen with all my heart."

The evening unfolded with stories that stretched the bounds of Sammy's imagination—tales of midnight rescues from precarious situations, daring encounters with venomous serpents, and the meticulous care bestowed upon injured wildlife. Each story painted a portrait of a man unafraid to challenge conventions in his pursuit of a greater purpose.

As the night deepened, Pitya led Sammy to a small, dimly lit room – a space that seemed to exist outside of time itself. There, amidst flickering candles and the faint scent of incense, rested a curious artefact – a meticulously cleaned buffalo skull, placed reverently at the centre of an intimate table setting.

"I found it during one of my jungle expeditions," Pitya explained casually, a mischievous glint in his eye. "A perfect addition to a candlelit dinner, don't you think?"

Sammy, already teetering on the edge of disbelief, excused himself with a stammered apology. The evening had pushed the limits of his comprehension, leaving him grappling with a reality that blurred the line between myth and the extraordinary.

Outside, the city of Pune hummed with life, its denizens unaware of the singular existence nestled within its midst. Pitya continued his nocturnal rituals, rubbing tobacco with practiced ease, answering calls for help. His life was a testament to the belief that true courage lies not in reckless abandon, but in a steadfast commitment to one's convictions.

In the days and years that followed, Pitya's legend grew. His animal welfare centre became a beacon of hope for creatures in distress, his name whispered in reverence by those who sought his aid. Through it all, he remained unchanged, a man whose eccentricities were matched only by his unwavering dedication to the creatures that shared his world.

As for Sammy, the memory of that evening lingered—the enduring allure of a man who dared to defy convention and embrace the extraordinary. In Pitya's world, the line between myth and reality blurred, a reminder that life's true wonders often lie beyond the boundaries of what is considered normal or expected.

Pitya lived a life guided by a deep respect for nature and its creatures. His unconventional choices and fearless pursuits underscored a belief in the intrinsic value of all life, regardless of its form or origin. Through his actions, he demonstrated that true courage lies in embracing empathy, challenging norms, and dedicating oneself to a cause that resonates deeply with the soul.

Chapter 9

The Vintage Studio

In the heart of Pune, nestled within the bustling Deccan Gymkhana area, lay the vibrant and chaotic Hongkong Lane. A narrow alley that seemed to pulse with life. Hongkong Lane was a treasure trove for the city's youth during the 1990s. Lined with tiny shops on either side, the lane was a haven for accessories: caps, bags, goggles, and more. The crowd barely fit in the crammed lane, yet the people thrived in this bustling atmosphere. The cacophony of bargaining filled the air, where a quoted price of 500 rupees often settled at a mere 50 bucks after a spirited negotiation. College students, brimming with the thrill of a good bargain, often spent their meagre pocket money here. They flocked to the lane for birthday gift shopping, to browse the latest trends, or simply to soak in the ambiance. The latest fashion trends, reflective of the era's pop culture, were born here. However, the advent of modern malls has since shrouded the glory of Hongkong Lane in the mists of nostalgia.

A unique allure of Hongkong Lane was its audio tape shops, tucked towards the end. These shops were among the few in the city that sold English music albums. A hot spot for the city's youth, these shops offered a personalised service: for just forty bucks, they would record a custom list of songs onto a cassette, ready the next day. This was a boon for music lovers who couldn't afford the pricey albums. Often, you'd see kids eagerly waiting with their song lists. Special recorded tapes of Grammy-winning songs were also a highlight, a coveted possession for any music aficionado.

Hongkong Lane was a vibrant corridor in the heart of Pune, adorned with some of the city's most popular hangouts. Among these was Lucky Restaurant, an Iranian food joint known for its aromatic dishes and nostalgic charm. Just as popular was the Good Luck Café, another Iranian establishment famous for its Bun Maska and Chai. These cafes were institutions in their own right, remaining open into the wee hours and often packed with students. Whether they were cramming for exams or unwinding from a night of partying, the students flocked to these pocket-friendly spots that had been beloved for generations.

Lucky Restaurant, however, wasn't as fortunate as its name suggested. It eventually fell to the relentless march of modernisation, replaced by a towering mall that overshadowed the memories of its once-popular fare. In contrast, Good Luck Café seemed to have been aptly named, continuing to stand proudly as a testament to the past, its walls whispering stories of yesteryear. For anyone who has studied in Pune during that era, a conversation about these two places is inevitable, a shared memory that bound them together. Even those who had moved away from the city or the country would make it a point to visit the café when back in town, eager to relive the nostalgia of their youth.

Strategically located, Hongkong Lane was flanked by seven single-screen movie theatres, adding to its allure. The Hindvijay, later renamed Natraj, and the Deccan Theatre were just next to the lane. A short walk away were Alka Talkies and Rahul Theatre; the latter known for screening English movies. Not far off, Mangala and Vijay theatres also drew crowds. Each cinema house had its unique charm and loyal patrons, making the area a hub for film enthusiasts.

Adding to the vibrancy of Hongkong Lane was its proximity to several prominent colleges. Modern College, Fergusson College, BMCC College, Garware College, and Agriculture College were all nearby, ensuring a constant buzz of student activity. The streets were alive with the chatter and footsteps of students, and every corner seemed to host a Vada Pav stall. Each vendor prided themselves on their unique recipe, and their stalls were perpetually surrounded by hungry scholars.

During the 1990s, the area around Hongkong Lane was a lively, dynamic place. The mix of culinary delights, cinematic experiences, and educational institutions created a microcosm of the city's youthful energy and cultural richness. The streets were always bustling, filled with laughter, debate, and the irresistible aroma of street food. It was a place where memories were made, friendships were forged, and the pulse of Pune's vibrant life could be felt in every corner.

The story of Abhay Ramchandra Ghorpade dates back to this era. He had just embarked on his journey as a Bachelor of Arts student at the prestigious Fergusson College. Abhay was born into a typical Puneri family in Pune's Mangalwar Peth, a name that in itself spoke volumes to any local. His father, Ramchandra Sadashiv Ghorpade, ran a small photo studio near Mandai (the oldest market in Pune), a legacy passed down from his father and beyond. This was perhaps Pune's oldest photo studio, proudly advertising 'since 1885'. The family dreamed of

Abhay continuing the tradition, but Abhay had other plans. Not that he knew exactly what he wanted, but he was keen to explore life on his own terms.

Short and lanky, with curly hair forming a perfect wave, a budding moustache, and a light beard, Abhay stood out with his fair complexion and unique charm. Physically light and agile, he always moved swiftly, though he missed the rhythm. He would easily get enamoured by the new things he saw and people he met. His aspiration to join Fergusson College was primarily to be a part of the pop culture around the college and the excitement it promised.

He had graduated from a Marathi medium school with flying colours and was thrilled to be admitted to one of the best arts colleges. However, on his first day, he did question his sense of fashion. Still carrying his old school bag and wearing khaki pants, he felt out of place among his fashionably dressed peers, many of whom may have shopped at Hongkong Lane, he thought.

Determined to fit in, Abhay made a mental note to update his wardrobe. Abhay cycled to college on a well-maintained but old-fashioned bicycle handed down from his father. Embarrassed by its outdated look, he parked it away from the college and walked through the main gate, hoping to blend in. His friendly nature and storytelling knack quickly earned him friends, particularly Ashwin, who owned a Luna moped. They often bunked classes to roam around the college road and Deccan Gymkhana, revelling in their newfound freedom. Learning to ride the Luna was a turning point for Abhay, thanks to Ashwin's generosity. Ten bucks' worth of petrol was enough to fuel their adventures, from dodging traffic cops to navigating without brakes when the cable broke.

Slowly, Abhay's style evolved. Neon laces from Hongkong Lane adorned his once-old-fashioned shoes. He replaced his school bag with a trendy backpack, and his khaki pants gave way to the latest jeans, aggressively bargained! Each visit to Hongkong Lane was a step towards a new Abhay, one who was embracing the pop culture and carving his own identity. The lane, with its chaotic charm and endless possibilities, became a symbol of his journey from a boy bound by tradition to a young man eager to write his own story.

Abhay's transformation wasn't just limited to his appearance. As he started to blend more with his college crowd, he began to delve into different aspects of life that he had never explored before. His academic pursuits at Fergusson College opened doors to new ideas and philosophies. Abhay found himself particularly drawn to literature and theatre. He spent hours in the college library, devouring books by Indian and Western authors alike. The world of words fascinated him, and he began to dream of becoming a writer someday, much to the chagrin of his father, who still hoped he would take over the family photo studio.

Abhay's love for reading was profound, yet he struggled with a lack of confidence when speaking English. Often, he would either remain silent or restrict himself to a few words, conscious of his limitations. However, Abhay possessed an unwavering eagerness to improve himself, never hesitating to embrace opportunities for learning and growth.

One day, while overhearing a conversation among his affluent friends about the year's Grammy winners, a name caught his attention: Tracy Chapman. The name resonated deeply with him, sparking a curiosity that he couldn't ignore. The very next day, brimming with enthusiasm, Abhay found himself standing outside a cassette shop, clutching a list of Tracy Chapman's songs. His excitement was palpable when he finally purchased the recorded tape, and he dashed home with a sense of urgency and delight.

Upon reaching home, Abhay played "Fast Car" on his father's old tape recorder, listening to it repeatedly, almost a hundred times. With each play, he meticulously transcribed the lyrics, writing down every word and committed them to memory. He practiced the pronunciation of each word diligently, turning this exercise into a labour of love.

What began with Tracy Chapman soon evolved into a cherished routine. Abhay's passion for music expanded as he delved into the works of new artists and explored various genres regularly. This practice brought about a significant transformation in him. He found himself confidently engaging in discussions about music with his friends, his command of the English language gradually improving with each conversation.

Abhay took immense pride in this personal achievement. Deep down, he knew that this pursuit of musical and linguistic excellence was something he would continue for life. The skills he developed not only bolstered his confidence but also enabled him to forge new friendships. Through his dedication and passion, Abhay discovered a lifelong joy that enriched his life and opened doors to new opportunities.

Today, Abhay stands as the proud proprietor of his family's venerable photo studio, yet he operates it on his own terms.

Not only is he one of the city's renowned photographers, but he has also orchestrated a stunning transformation of the old studio. A few years ago, the studio underwent a metamorphosis; while the walls remained the same, the infusion of vibrant new colours and state-of-the-art equipment created a mesmerising blend of the old and the new. Abhay's youthful charm and infectious happiness remain undiminished. Often found humming a tune, lost in his own world, he exudes a sense of contentment and fulfilment.

In moments of reflection, Abhay contemplates the journey that led him to this point. His mind drifts back, like a fast car from Tracy Chapman's song, to a pivotal memory.

After immersing himself in Tracy's music for a month, Abhay found himself wandering through Hongkong Lane, where he bought a Metallica-embossed baseball cap. The cap cost him 200 rupees, a price he begrudgingly paid, though he was pleased with the purchase. Determined to showcase his new cap, he borrowed Ashwin's Luna and sped to a nearby Shirole petrol pump. Handing over 10 rupees to the attendant, Abhay noticed the attendant's gaze fixed on his cap, accompanied by a bemused smile.

"Nice cap, I like it," the attendant remarked, his eyes twinkling. Abhay smiled back, feeling a surge of pride. Then came the unexpected question, "Will you give it to me?" Abhay was stunned, thrown off balance by the audacity of the request. Abhay was at a loss for words. The attendant continued, "Sir (a long pause), you need a lot of courage to give that expensive cap to me!"

This encounter marked a turning point in Abhay's life. In that moment, he realised the shallowness of materialism and the profound peace that comes from letting go. We often become attached to insignificant possessions, forgetting that true joy lies in the people we love, the art we cherish, and the passions that drive us.

From the bustling lanes of Hong Kong to his now renovated and thriving studio, Abhay's journey has been nothing short of rewarding. The transformation of his studio mirrors his own inner growth, a testament to the realisation that what truly matters are the intangible joys of life.

The Metallica cap made its way onto the attendant's head that day, giving a new purpose to Abhay's life.

Chapter 10

A True Friend

———— ❈ ————

"Click!" The delightful sound of the mobile camera flash filled the air, capturing a momentous occasion on Ritesh's brand new iPhone 15 Pro. A sense of pride radiated from his face as he eagerly shared the photo with his colleagues at Aba's Tapri situated near by his office. A cosy paan & tea stall situated near the impressive edifices that housed renowned corporate giants. Baner, an up-and-coming area in Pune, had swiftly transformed into a bustling hub of commercial complexes and IT companies, attracting ambitious professionals like Ritesh.

Having completed his engineering degree from the prestigious COEP, Ritesh had initially found himself on the path of engineering at the urging of his parents. However, it was his specialisation in robotics that truly ignited his passion. A natural tinkerer at heart, Ritesh had always been fascinated by the intricacies of technology. Born and raised in an upper-middle-class family in Pune, he had the privilege of attending some of the city's finest educational institutions. While his parents held onto their traditional values, they were also open to the winds of change brought by the wave of westernisation that gently embraced Pune's Marathi culture. Ritesh, too, believed in adapting to the shifting times while honouring his roots, and his new mobile phone symbolised his willingness to embrace the modern world. It was a much-deserved treat, funded by the satisfactory bonus he had received at work.

Within the office, Ritesh was renowned as the life and soul of every party. His infectious energy and natural charisma made him the go-to person for organising and energising office events. Colleagues eagerly anticipated his lively presence and dynamic leadership. Meanwhile, unbeknownst to his parents, Ritesh had formed a beautiful connection with Priya, an enchanting young girl hailing from an upper-middle-class Brahmin family. Their relationship epitomised the harmonious fusion of two distinct worlds. Ritesh, a Konknastha Brahmin, lovingly referred to as "KoBra" among his friends, found himself entwined with Priya, a Deshastha Brahmin, affectionately referred to as "DeBra." Their love story exemplified the perfect blending of cultures and traditions, creating a unique bond that resonated with both their hearts and souls.

As Ritesh pulled his red Maruti Baleno from the parking lot, he was looking forward to meeting up with Priya near Fergusson College, their usual spot - Crumbs. A small yet homely place to have a coffee and something fresh from the bakery to eat. They were often seen sitting here, and the staff knew them very well. While Ritesh's life was the ideal life one could dream of, on the other end of the spectrum was Jagdish.

Jagdish Shripad Apte, affectionately now known as Jaggu Da, bore the marks of a life lived on the edge of hardship and resilience. His face, weathered by time and lined with the stories of battles fought and won, spoke volumes of the challenges he had overcome. Each scar etched into his visage was a testament to his unwavering determination and inner strength.

As he entered his 60th year, Jaggu Da's countenance carried the weight of his experiences, a silent narrative of triumph in the face of adversity. Despite the hardships he had endured, there was a sense of victory that radiated from within him, a testament to his indomitable spirit.

His athletic frame, standing tall at 6.2 feet, bore the physical marks of a life lived with vigour and determination. Though age had begun to slow his movements, there was still an undeniable strength in the way he carried himself, a quiet confidence that spoke of battles won and challenges overcome.

Jaggu Da's distinctive style was an extension of his persona, a reflection of his inner resilience and strength. Clad in crisp white attire, he exuded an aura of invincibility, his choice of clothing adding to his mystique. With his hair now almost grey and his white moustache impeccably groomed in a handlebar style, he commanded attention wherever he went, a figure of quiet authority and strength.

His presence was akin to that of a superhero stepping out of the pages of a comic book, his all-white ensemble serving as a symbol of his unwavering resolve and inner fortitude. With each step, Jaggu Da carried with him the weight of his experiences, a reminder that even in the face of life's greatest challenges, it is possible to emerge stronger and more resilient than ever before. His transformation from Jagdish to Jaggu to Jaggu Da resembled a captivating storyline from a movie. It was evident that his life had been anything but ordinary.

Every morning, like clockwork, Jaggu Da would make his way to Aba's Tapri, a ritual that had become as ingrained in his routine as the rising of the sun. With a slow, deliberate pace, he would approach the counter with a sense of grace that belied the hardships he had endured. As his palm met the familiar surface of Aba's counter, no words were exchanged, yet a silent understanding passed between them, a connection forged through years of shared moments and unspoken gestures.

For Aba, Jaggu Da's daily visit was a bittersweet reminder of a fateful day many years ago, a day that had changed the course of his life forever. Abhay, aka Aba, had been a young college student. Yet, despite his academic interest, he found himself adrift in a sea of uncertainty, unsure of how to navigate the challenges that lay ahead.

A friendly tap on his shoulder, the sound of laughter ringing in his ears as he turned to face Jagdish, his saviour and lifelong friend. With a simple gesture, Jagdish offered Aba a cup of cutting chai, a small act of kindness that would spark a friendship destined to withstand the test of time. Jagdish possessed a rare gift for understanding people, for seeing beyond the surface to the heart of a person's true nature. He recognised in Aba a kindred spirit, a fellow traveller on the journey of life, and vowed to guide him through the challenges that lay ahead. Aba became a member of Jagdish's gang.

Amidst the triumphs, there lingered a shadow of the past, a haunting reminder of the day Jagdish's life took a tragic turn. Faced with a moment of violence, Jagdish had acted out of instinct, defending Aba from harm, at the cost of his own freedom. Sentenced to thirty years in prison, Jagdish bore his punishment with stoic dignity, never once betraying the secret he had sworn to protect.

For Aba, the years passed in a blur of longing and regret. His visits to Jagdish's prison cell were a bittersweet reminder of the debt he could never repay. And yet, despite the distance that separated them, their bond remained unbroken, a silent testament to the enduring power of friendship.

As Jagdish emerged from prison, his spirit unbroken by the passage of time, Aba welcomed him back into his life with open arms, grateful for the chance to once again share in his friend's presence. And though the years had changed them both, their bond remained as strong as ever, a beacon of hope in a world often fraught with darkness.

Every morning, as Jaggu Da stood before Aba's counter, a silent tribute to the enduring power of friendship, Aba couldn't help but marvel at the twists and turns that had brought them to this moment. And as they exchanged their daily ritual of nods and smiles, Aba knew that, no matter what challenges lay ahead, they would face them together, bound by a friendship that transcended time and space.

The encounter at the café had left Ritesh shaken to his core. What began as a casual moment of amusement, capturing a photo of a "filmy guy", Jaggu Da, on his phone, had spiralled into a chilling reality. Little did he and Priya realise, their seemingly innocent banter had drawn the attention of the enigmatic figure known as Jaggu Da.

As Jaggu Da loomed in the background, his presence unnoticed until it was too late, Ritesh felt a chill run down his spine. The weight of Jaggu Da's gaze bore down on him like a heavy cloak, suffocating him with a sense of dread that refused to dissipate.

Hurriedly taking Priya's hand, Ritesh fled from the café, his mind racing with questions and fear. Dropping her home, he found himself unable to shake the image of Jaggu Da from his mind, the tall figure haunting his thoughts like a ghost in the night.

Sleep eluded him as he tossed and turned, tormented by the relentless presence of Jaggu Da in his mind's eye. And as dawn broke, he found himself drawn, once again, to the familiar comfort of Aba's Tapri, seeking solace in the routine of his morning tea and smoke.

But even here, Jaggu Da's shadow loomed large, his slight grin a silent reminder of the unease that had taken hold of Ritesh's life. Desperate for answers, he confided in his friends, their curiosity piqued by the mystery that had ensnared their friend.

Determined to uncover the truth, Abhijit led the charge, his keen intellect driving him to seek out information on Jaggu Da. With a mixture of trepidation and resolve, he embarked on a journey to uncover the identity of the mysterious figure who had infiltrated his life.

Their quest led them to Aba's Tapri once more, where Aba greeted them with a knowing smile as if he had been expecting them. Showing him the photo of Jaggu Da, Ritesh pleaded for answers, his heart pounding in anticipation.

But Aba's response only deepened the mystery as he revealed the name Jagdish Shripad Apte - a name shrouded in infamy, a name that sent shivers down their spines, knowing about a leader of the gang, a don! Armed with this newfound knowledge, he delved deeper into Jaggu Da's past, uncovering a dark history stained with violence and incarceration.

As the truth began to unravel, fear gripped him like a vice, his mind racing with questions and doubts. Ritesh's heart raced as he recounted the unsettling encounter with Jaggu Da to Priya, his voice tinged with a mixture of fear and determination. Sensing the gravity of the situation, he pleaded with Priya to refrain from meeting until he could unravel the mystery that had enveloped his life.

Despite his best efforts to carry on as normal, the spectre of Jaggu Da loomed over him like a dark cloud, casting a shadow of unease wherever he went. With each passing day, Ritesh felt the weight of his burden grow heavier, his resolve tested by the relentless pursuit of the enigmatic figure who seemed to be watching his every move.

With a newfound determination, Ritesh declared his intention to confront Jaggu Da head-on to his friends. His voice rang with defiance as he vowed to put an end to the torment that had consumed him. Ritesh stormed out of the restaurant where they were having dinner, realising that his follower would be around, his footsteps echoing in the silence that followed.

Outside, Jaggu Da stood waiting, his presence a chilling reminder of the danger that lurked in the shadows. With a swift motion, he seized Ritesh by the collar, lifting him effortlessly into the air with a strength that seemed otherworldly. In that moment, Ritesh felt a surge of fear grip him, his mind racing as he braced himself for what seemed like an inevitable end.

But as Jaggu Da's hand moved to reveal its hidden contents, Ritesh's world came to a standstill. Time seemed to slow to a crawl as he stared into the depths of Jaggu Da's eyes, seeing not a threat but a glimmer of something else – a flicker of understanding, perhaps, or even compassion.

And then, in a blink of an eye, it was over. Jaggu Da released Ritesh from his grip, his hand withdrawing to reveal not a weapon, but a simple bouquet of red roses. Confusion washed over Ritesh as he struggled to make sense of what had just transpired, his mind reeling from the whirlwind of emotions that had engulfed him.

With a deep, resonant voice, Jaggu Da uttered a simple yet profound "Thank you" as he handed over the bouquet of red roses to Ritesh. Shock reverberated through Ritesh's being, his mouth agape in disbelief at the unexpected gesture. Before he could muster a response, Jaggu Da swiftly pressed the bouquet into his hands and turned away, disappearing into the night.

In that moment, Ritesh realised that perhaps Jaggu Da was not the enemy he had feared, but a fellow traveller on the journey of life – a soul burdened by his own trials and tribulations, seeking solace in the fleeting moments of connection that bound them together.

As Ritesh stood there, the weight of his fear lifting from his shoulders, he felt a sense of peace wash over him. And though the mysteries of Jaggu Da's past remained unsolved, Ritesh knew that, whatever the future held, he would face it with courage and resolve.

The mystery of Jaggu Da's gesture lingered in the air, casting a shadow over his thoughts. What secrets lay hidden beneath the surface, waiting to be uncovered?

Aba's smile held a hint of mystery as he reflected on his recent encounter with Jaggu Da. The old memories intertwined with the present, creating a tapestry of emotions that Aba couldn't quite decipher.

In their clandestine meeting the night before, Jaggu Da had revealed a secret to Aba that had weighed heavily on his mind for years. He confided in Aba about the fateful incident in prison where a brutal encounter with the new jailer had left him battered and broken. The blow to his head had stolen something precious from him – his ability to see colours.

For Jaggu Da, a life devoid of colours was akin to living in a perpetual twilight where shades of grey painted his world with melancholy. He had spent decades wandering through the monochrome landscape of his existence, longing for the vibrant hues that had once illuminated his path.

But fate works in mysterious ways, and on that fateful day, when Ritesh captured his picture with his new phone, something miraculous happened. The flash of the camera ignited a spark within Jaggu Da's eyes, awakening his dormant senses and restoring the colours that had long eluded him.

From that moment onward, Jaggu Da was on a quest to find Ritesh to express his gratitude for the gift of sight that had been returned to him. In a world where reality often blurred the lines between truth and illusion, Jaggu Da's journey was a testament to the transformative power of unexpected encounters and the profound impact they could have on one's life.

As Aba pondered Jaggu Da's story, he realised that not everything we see or experience is true. Sometimes, the most profound truths lie hidden beneath the surface, waiting to be uncovered by those who dare to venture into the depths of the human experience. And in Jaggu Da's journey, Aba found a glimmer of hope, a reminder that even in the darkest of times, there is always light waiting to be discovered.

Chapter 11

Culinary Delight

Mandar Gore was a successful IT professional, a shining beacon of the middle-class that dared to dream big and leave the shackles of convention behind in pursuit of new horizons. Born and raised in the vibrant city of Pune in Kothrud, he embodied the values and aspirations of his community.

Mandar moved into a swanky apartment in a gated community shortly after he came back to India. Married to Seema, an IT professional herself, their story began in Silicon Valley, where Mandar was working at a tech company in Cupertino at the start of his career. They met, fell in love, and eventually decided to marry. After the birth of their daughters, Jai and Jui, they chose to return to India. Mandar firmly believed in the importance of staying close to one's motherland and parents, especially as they aged. No amount of money could replace the satisfaction of being near his parents when they needed him most. A firm practitioner of cultural values and a believer in hard work and familial ties, Mandar was a true Punekar. His parents, wife, and children were proud of him, and to their neighbours, Mandar was the true epitome of success.

Weekends in the Gore household were a sight to behold. Mandar, despite a gruelling work week, could be seen brimming with energy, playing with his daughters in the society park or swimming with them. The simplicity of his daughters' names, chosen as per their sun signs and reflecting the names of flowers, was a testament to his belief in keeping life uncomplicated. He shunned the trend of fancy and difficult names, preferring those that were easy to pronounce and meaningful. This philosophy extended to his professional life as well, where he was known for writing simplified code for complex processes. His boss and colleagues admired his calm demeanour and problem-solving skills under tight deadlines. These traits had propelled him up the organisational ladder, earning him well-deserved recognition and respect.

Mandar's father had dedicated his life to working as a clerk in the Municipal Corporation with the sole mission of providing the best education for his only son. Today, he is a proud father, asking for nothing more than the joy of seeing Mandar's success. Observing Mandar, one could see a fine blend of the old and the new. With a decent haircut reminiscent of his school days, a well-shaved face, and a neatly trimmed moustache, Mandar's appearance reflected a balance between tradition and modernity. His choice of T-shirts and jeans showed a willingness to adapt to new trends, but within limits. Despite being well-travelled, having a good friend circle, and an active social network, Mandar had no vices. A jovial individual, he preferred to stay home and spend quality time with his family.

Seema, a successful professional in her own right, had given up her job a few years ago to focus on their daughters and care for her ageing in-laws. The family had consciously avoided the growing culture of day-care, believing in the value of grandparents' presence in instilling cultural values in the children. Despite her hectic days, Seema found peace in managing her duties. Whether it was the kids' schoolwork, their projects, or taking them to their classes, she did everything with a smile. Mandar was especially proud of Seema, finding contentment in their marriage.

After Seema took on the role of the "CEO" at home, she discovered a passion for culinary arts. She loved making various Indian dishes for her family, and her in-laws never complained about the extended daily menu. As the years passed, she honed her cooking skills. Mandar, recognising her talent early on, encouraged her to pursue her passion. The support from her in-laws, Mandar, and their daughters fuelled her culinary endeavours. She found immense joy in seeing Mandar relish her food and appreciate her efforts. He continually motivated her to experiment with dishes from different regions, always eager to be the first to try her new creations. While her in-laws offered constructive feedback on the spice or salt levels, Mandar's unwavering enthusiasm made Seema happy.

One evening, as Mandar returned home after a particularly long day at work, he was greeted by the mouth-watering aroma of Seema's latest culinary creation. The children were playing in the living room, their laughter echoing through the apartment. Mandar's heart swelled with happiness as he stepped inside. The cosy, warm atmosphere was a stark contrast to the sterile, high-pressure environment of his office.

As the family sat down to eat, Mandar looked around the table, feeling a profound sense of gratitude. He knew that his parents, who had sacrificed so much for him, were content. His wife was flourishing in her role, and his children were growing up in a loving, nurturing environment. It was a life he had dreamed of and worked hard to achieve. His journey from a middle-class upbringing in Pune to a successful career in Silicon Valley, and back to Pune, where he had built a life grounded in family values and cultural traditions, seemed surreal. He had seen the world, experienced the highs and lows of a demanding career, and yet, it was the simple, everyday moments with his family that brought him the greatest joy.

The next day at work, Mandar was approached by his boss. "Mandar, we have a new project coming up, and it's going to require a lot of time and effort. I know it's a lot to ask, but I believe you're the best person for the job."

Mandar considered the offer carefully. The project would be a significant career milestone, but it would also mean less time with his family. He thought about Seema and the girls, his parents, and the life they had built together.

"Thank you for considering me, boss," Mandar replied. "But I need to balance my professional and personal life. I can't take on something that will take me away from my family for too long." His boss looked surprised but nodded in understanding. "I respect that, Mandar. It's rare to find someone who values family as much as you do."

As Mandar walked back to his desk, he felt a sense of peace with his decision. He had always believed that success was not just about professional achievements, but also about maintaining strong, loving relationships and staying true to one's values.

That evening, as Mandar played with his daughters and later enjoyed a quiet dinner with Seema, he knew he had made the right choice. Life was not just about the next big project or promotion; it was about the moments of joy, the bonds of family, and the satisfaction of living a life grounded in love and integrity.

One particularly memorable weekend, Mandar and Seema decided to take their daughters on a surprise trip to Mahabaleshwar. The scenic hill station, with its lush greenery and strawberry farms, was a perfect getaway. The girls squealed with delight as they drove through the winding roads, the cool breeze rustling their hair.

At the resort, they spent the days exploring nature trails, boating on the serene Venna Lake, and picking fresh strawberries from the farms. Mandar watched his daughters with a heart full of contentment. He and Seema shared moments of quiet joy, watching the sunset over the hills, feeling a deeper connection to each other and their family.

In the evenings, they gathered around a campfire, roasting potatoes and sharing stories. Mandar told his daughters tales of his own childhood, of the times he spent with their grandfather, and the lessons he learned. Seema talked about her love for cooking and how it brought her closer to her own mother. These stories created a tapestry of memories, weaving the past with the present and instilling in Jai and Jui a sense of belonging and heritage.

That night, Seema's heart skipped a beat as she recalled Mandar's confession. She couldn't believe that he had kept such a significant detail hidden from her all these years. Tears welled up in her eyes as she realised the depth of his sacrifice and the extent to which he had gone to ensure her happiness.

"Mandar," she whispered, her voice choked with emotion. "Why didn't you tell me?"

Mandar gently wiped away her tears, his eyes filled with love and sincerity. "I didn't want to burden you with my problems, Seema. I knew how much joy cooking brought you, and I didn't want my inability to taste to dampen that. Seeing you happy was all that mattered to me."

Seema was overwhelmed by a flood of emotions. She had always admired Mandar's selflessness and dedication to their family, but this revelation took her admiration to a whole new level. Despite facing such a significant setback, he had never complained or sought sympathy. Instead, he had continued to support her, encouraging her culinary pursuits, and celebrating her successes.

"I don't know what to say, Mandar," Seema said, her voice trembling. "You've been carrying this burden alone for so long, and I had no idea."

Mandar smiled, his eyes shining with warmth. "It's not a burden, Seema. It's a part of who I am. A small accident a few years back took my sense of taste away, but that does not define who I am. What matters is that we're together as a family, and nothing can take that away from us."

Seema wrapped her arms around Mandar, holding him tightly as if afraid to let go. In that moment, she felt an overwhelming sense of gratitude for the man who had been her rock, her pillar of strength through every twist and turn of their journey together.

Chapter 12

The Unforgettable Auto Rickshaw Ride

One of the prominent and unmistakable sights in Pune is the swarm of black and yellow creatures that irritatingly roar through the streets and narrow lanes. These ubiquitous three-wheeled vehicles, known as auto rickshaws, are a hallmark of the city's bustling life. With their distinctive colour scheme, they dart in and out of traffic, their engines buzzing with a persistent, droning hum. The auto rickshaws, often adorned with vibrant stickers and sometimes bedecked with colourful decorations, serve as a lifeline for many commuters, weaving through the city's organised chaos with practiced ease. Despite their small size, their presence is loud and inescapable, a constant reminder of the pulse and pace of Pune.

Driven by expert hands, these auto rickshaws can be seen squeezing through the narrowest of gaps, honking their way through the traffic-clogged streets. The drivers, with their remarkable agility, navigate the labyrinthine roads, often taking shortcuts only they seem to know. The interiors of these autos are a microcosm of local culture, with Bollywood posters, deity stickers, and often a small shrine on the dashboard. Passengers hop on and off with practiced ease, engaging in brief yet lively haggling over fares.

The auto rickshaws are not just a mode of transport, but a symbol of Pune's dynamic energy. They reflect the city's character – vibrant, relentless, and full of life. As they roar past the city's landmarks, from the historic Shaniwar Wada to the bustling FC Road, their presence is a constant thread through the fabric of Pune's everyday existence. Whether it's the early morning rush to work or the late-night return from a social gathering, these three-wheeled chariots are always on the move, embodying the spirit of the city that never seems to slow down.

If you have regularly travelled in an auto rickshaw in Pune, you would know the pain it takes to secure a ride. It's not because the autos are always busy, but because of the drivers' unpredictable and often uncooperative attitudes. These drivers seem to embody everything that Pune means – vibrant yet capricious, bustling yet unyielding. It is not uncommon for a commuter to request a ride from four or five auto drivers before finding one willing to go to a particular destination. On a lucky day, you might find a willing driver after only three or four attempts.

The responses from these drivers often defy any reasonable expectations of human behaviour. It sometimes seems as if their primary goal on the road is to deny rides to prospective passengers. As you utter the name of your desired destination, you can witness a range of facial reactions that could rival those of the best character actors. Their expressions can convey an exaggerated sense of disdain, incredulity, or outright refusal, leaving you to wonder what you might have done to deserve such a reaction. It's as if asking for a ride is an insult, and you begin to question what planet these drivers come from and who granted them the authority to deny passengers so whimsically.

The destination you request plays a crucial role in this negotiation. Some drivers are on the lookout for longer trips that promise higher fares, while others prefer short, quick rides. The moment you reveal where you need to go, you can see the drivers mentally calculating the feasibility and desirability of the trip. If your destination doesn't meet their unspoken criteria, their faces will contort in exaggerated disappointment or annoyance. It's an experience that often leaves passengers feeling perplexed and frustrated.

One can't help but wonder why these drivers are even in the business of providing rides if they seem so averse to taking passengers. Their mood can swing the outcome of your request significantly, making the process feel like a game of chance rather than a straightforward transaction. Sometimes, the refusal feels personal, as if you have somehow offended them by merely stating your destination.

Indeed, securing an auto rickshaw ride in Pune requires a combination of persistence, luck, and the ability to navigate the whims and moods of the drivers. It's a dance of negotiation that every commuter must learn, adding another layer of complexity to the already vibrant and chaotic life of the city.

Most of the time, it is also the look of the passengers that may decide their fate when trying to get a ride. If the passengers appear old, there is a higher chance that you might secure a ride, as this sight might touch the empathy cord of the driver. The drivers often assess potential passengers with a scrutinising eye, making quick judgements about who they are willing to transport.

For couples, the driver will be very particular about whether they are willing to pay the expected fare and if they have the exact change. This negotiation can sometimes feel like a delicate dance, with the driver weighing his options based on the perceived hassle or convenience. Ladies may also find it slightly easier to get a ride as drivers might be more inclined to assist them, perhaps out of a sense of chivalry or cultural norms.

If you are a solo passenger, however, the process might be more challenging. It can take a while until a driver offers you a ride, as solo passengers are often seen as less lucrative. The driver's decision might hinge on the perceived distance of the trip or the likelihood of picking up additional passengers along the way.

When it comes to passengers with luggage, the situation becomes even more complex. If you have bags or other items, be prepared for the driver to notify you about extra charges. This is almost a given, as the additional hassle of accommodating luggage in the cramped confines of an auto rickshaw is seen as an opportunity to charge more. Also, be ready to treat yourself to the driver's colourful vocabulary if you attempt to stuff the luggage into the tight spaces without his assistance or approval. The interaction can quickly turn sour, with the driver expressing his displeasure in no uncertain terms.

The dynamic between passenger and driver in Pune is a nuanced one, where factors such as age, gender, group size, and even the presence of luggage play significant roles in the negotiation for a ride. It's a system that operates on unspoken rules and instinctive judgements, adding another layer of complexity to the already intricate tapestry of life in the city. Each interaction is a small drama, unfolding with its own set of challenges and negotiations, making the simple act of securing an auto rickshaw ride a unique and sometimes exasperating experience.

It often feels as if there's a hidden "Dummy's Guide to Rejecting Passengers in 100 Ways" that auto rickshaw drivers in Pune must be studying and mastering before they hit the roads. Their skill in turning down prospective passengers is almost an art form, and they seem to have an arsenal of techniques at their disposal. Here are the top rejection modes that passengers frequently encounter:

The No-Word-But-Facial-Expression Denial

This breed of drivers relies solely on facial expressions to convey their refusal. Without uttering a single word, they can communicate a resounding "NO" through a repertoire of grimaces, frowns, and eye rolls. The range and subtlety of these expressions are too vast to be documented comprehensively. An expert passenger, seasoned by years of navigating the auto rickshaw scene, can gauge these expressions from a hundred metres away. However, for the uninitiated, this silent refusal can be bewildering and leaves one pondering what went wrong. This method of rejection is particularly enigmatic as it leaves no room for negotiation or understanding, making you wonder if you ever stood a chance.

The One-Word Denial

In this mode, the driver doesn't waste time on elaborate refusals. A single, curt word is all it takes: "No." Delivered with a tone that brooks no argument, this type of rejection is swift and unambiguous. It's as if the driver has an internal quota of words he's willing to spend on passengers, and "No" is the most economical choice. This method can be jarring in its bluntness but at least provides a clear, if disappointing, answer. The brevity of this interaction often leaves passengers with little to respond to, making it one of the most efficient rejection techniques.

The Lengthy Discussion and Denial at the End

This method can be the most frustrating for passengers. The driver engages you in a detailed conversation about your destination, the route, the fare, and possibly even the weather, only to decline the ride after you think you've reached an understanding. This drawn-out process raises your hopes, making the eventual denial feel like a rug being pulled out from under you. The conversation might go through multiple stages, including seemingly earnest questions and nods of understanding, before culminating in a firm "No" or a sudden change of heart. It's a tactic that tests your patience and resilience, often leaving you more exasperated than you would be with a quicker rejection.

The Ignorant Denial

In this mode, the driver simply ignores your request altogether. You might stand there, repeatedly stating your destination while the driver stares ahead, fiddles with something in the auto, or pretends not to hear you. This technique is particularly infuriating because it robs you of the chance to even register a response. It's as if you've become invisible, and your request is deemed unworthy of acknowledgement. This silent treatment can feel dismissive and degrading, leaving you standing there unsure whether to persist or move on to the next auto in hopes of better luck.

These rejection techniques add another layer of complexity to the already challenging task of securing an auto rickshaw ride in Pune. Each encounter is a unique test of patience, resilience and, sometimes, creativity as you navigate the intricate dance of negotiation with these masters of denial.

Busting these myths, Sudhir had one auto rickshaw ride that gave him a life lesson and shattered his preconceived notions about auto drivers. Contrary to his belief that they were uniformly uncooperative, this experience proved that humanity is still alive, though it may be found sparingly.

One sweltering afternoon, Sudhir found himself in desperate need of a ride. After a series of rejections that tested his patience, he approached yet another auto driver with a sense of resignation. To his surprise, the driver not only agreed to take him to his destination but did so with a warm smile and genuine kindness that was rare in Sudhir's experience. The driver, a young man with a sharp look, welcomed Sudhir into his auto and greeted him with a warm "Namaskar".

Sudhir was enamoured by what he saw. The driver was a picture of immaculate presentation, wearing a pristine white shirt and white pants. Each fold showcased the crease of meticulously ironed clothes, highlighting the driver's attention to detail and pride in his appearance. The shirt was neatly tucked into the pants, and despite their weathered state, his black shoes were polished and gleaming, reflecting the afternoon sunlight.

He was clean-shaven, with a neatly trimmed moustache and well-maintained hair, presenting a dignified and composed demeanour. The driver's appearance reminded Sudhir of Jitendra, the iconic Bollywood actor known for his elegance and charm in yesteryear films. This unexpected resemblance brought a nostalgic smile to Sudhir's face.

The auto rickshaw itself was a testament to the driver's dedication and care. The interiors were kept remarkably clean and tastefully decorated, creating a pleasant and inviting atmosphere. Cushions covered the seats, providing a comfortable ride, and the dashboard featured small, thoughtful decorations. A miniature deity idol was placed on the dashboard, adorned with fresh flowers, adding a touch of spirituality and warmth.

A small but well-maintained music system played soft, melodious tunes, enhancing the overall experience. The subtle fragrance of incense wafted through the air, blending harmoniously with the music and creating a serene ambiance amidst the city's chaos. The auto rickshaw's exterior was equally well-kept, free of the usual dents and scratches, and its paint shone with a well-maintained lustre.

As they navigated through Pune's bustling streets, the driver shared stories from his life, painting a picture of the challenges and joys he faced every day. He spoke of his family, his struggles to make ends meet, and the simple pleasures that kept him going. It became clear to Sudhir that this man's seemingly endless patience and goodwill stemmed from a deep well of personal resilience and empathy.

Sudhir was struck by the driver's perspective on life. Despite the hardships, he maintained an unwavering commitment to treating his passengers with respect and kindness. The driver explained that he viewed his work not just as a means of earning a livelihood, but as an opportunity to connect with people and make their day a little better, even if only in small ways.

This ride was more than just a trip from one place to another; it was a journey into the heart of what it means to be human. The driver's humility, wisdom, and compassion left a lasting impression on Sudhir. It was a powerful reminder that, despite the many frustrations he had faced, there were still individuals who embodied the best of humanity.

This experience dismantled Sudhir's belief that all auto drivers were indifferent or unkind. He realised that while negative experiences were often more memorable, they did not represent the whole picture. There were still good people out there, quietly making a difference in their own small ways. This ride reaffirmed Sudhir's faith in humanity, teaching him that kindness could be found in the most unexpected places, even on the bustling streets of Pune.

"Happy morning," Sudhir said to the auto driver as he took yet another auto rickshaw ride to his office. This simple greeting had become a habit, a small but meaningful ritual that set a positive tone for his day.

Sudhir had learned an important lesson from his memorable encounter with the impeccably dressed and kind-hearted auto driver. He realised that greeting people costs nothing but can make a significant difference in how interactions unfold. A simple "happy morning" can brighten someone's day and pave the way for a more pleasant exchange.

Most importantly, Sudhir had come to appreciate the power of empathy. The driver's kindness and willingness to share his life stories had taught Sudhir that everyone is fighting their own battles, often invisible to others. Showing empathy and understanding can forge meaningful connections and remind us of our shared humanity.

Each ride was now an opportunity to practice these lessons, and Sudhir was determined to make the most of it.

Chapter 13

Vibrant Jignesh

Jignesh was a man of distinctive appearance and a vibrant personality. At 30 years old, he stood at five foot four, a diminutive figure that belied his larger-than-life character. His physical appearance, with a rounded and slightly chubby build, was a sharp contrast to his flamboyant fashion choices.

Jignesh's hair was meticulously trimmed and copiously oiled with Kesh Kala, a traditional hair oil that gave it a glossy sheen. He often styled it with a sharp parting, flattening it to the left side of his head. However, what truly caught one's attention were his shirts. They were a riot of colours and prints, reflecting his love for vividness and vibrancy.

Some of his shirts were blaring and eye-catching, featuring bold patterns and contrasting hues. Others seemed to sing a duet with their playful motifs, incorporating musical notes, instruments, or even lyrics. And then there were the shirts that transported one to a serene beach with their scenic prints of palm trees, waves, and sunsets.

Despite his unique attire, Jignesh's most notable accessory was his golden retro spectacle frame. Oversized for his face, it resembled those worn by the "lalas" (rich merchants) depicted in old Bollywood movies. It added an element of nostalgia to his appearance and, at times, it almost seemed as if Jignesh himself had stepped out of a bygone era.

Jignesh's colourful character extended beyond his clothing and accessories. He was always seen with a warm smile on his face, radiating positivity and joy. His eyes sparkled with an infectious enthusiasm, inviting others to join in his zest for life. His slow-paced walk had an underlying rhythm, as if there were invisible beats playing, and Jignesh was gracefully swaying to their tune.

His colleagues at the office were fond of his presence, appreciating the positive energy he brought with him. Whether it was his humming or his vibrant wardrobe, Jignesh had a way of brightening up the workplace. His colleagues admired his authenticity and found comfort in his unwavering cheerfulness.

Jignesh was a true embodiment of self-expression and individuality. His appearance might have seemed like a paradox, with his mismatched attire and physical attributes, but it only added to his charm. Jignesh's colourful persona and genuine smile made him a memorable figure in the lives of those who crossed his path.

Though Jignesh had left his hometown of Valsad behind, the memories of his traditional family and the quaint charm of the place remained etched in his heart. Valsad, nestled in the coastal region of Gujarat, is a town steeped in rich cultural heritage and vibrant traditions.

Jignesh's family had deep roots in Valsad, known for their business acumen and close-knit community. Every visit to his ancestral home was filled with warmth and laughter as relatives gathered under the shade of a banyan tree in their angan, sharing stories and savouring homemade delicacies.

The aroma of freshly brewed chai mixed with the tantalising scents of Gujarati snacks created an ambiance that was uniquely Valsadi. The bustling markets offered a plethora of colourful textiles, intricate embroidery, and traditional handicrafts, reflecting the region's artistic spirit.

In the evenings, the air resonated with the melodious tunes of traditional folk music and the rhythmic clapping of garba dancers. Jignesh's family, deeply rooted in their cultural heritage, celebrated every festival with immense fervour, their homes adorned with vibrant decorations and festive lights.

Despite the enchantment of his hometown, Jignesh's free-spirited nature often clashed with his family's traditional values. They held onto the belief that marriage and settling down were the cornerstones of a fulfilling life. In their eyes, Jignesh's eccentric personality clashed with the conservative ideals they held dear.

With every passing visit, his family's hopes for him to find a suitable bride intensified. Relatives would arrange meetings with potential matches, emphasising the importance of preserving their cultural lineage. However, Jignesh found it challenging to connect with the women presented to him. Their expectations clashed with his desire for a partner who would understand and support his hidden passion.

What hidden passion?

Of course, Jignesh did not have an answer, and that was his whole worry.

Jignesh's life in Mumbai was a whirlwind of creativity and ambition. With a dream to make a colourful career, he landed himself a client servicing job at a leading advertising agency. As an advertising professional, he thrived on the fast-paced nature of the industry, constantly seeking new ways to captivate audiences and bring ideas to life.

However, Jignesh's days were often accompanied by a sense of longing, a feeling that something was missing. He couldn't shake the feeling that his life lacked a deeper purpose, a true connection that went beyond the confines of his career.

While Jignesh pondered about the direction his life had taken, he was still unsure of what he was meant to be in this world. Each morning, he woke up with a hazy memory of the previous night, and as he looked at his short and chubby figure in the mirror, he felt a mix of amusement and astonishment. However, he embraced his unique identity and continued to express himself through his choice of clothing and his love for music.

Sitting in his bean bag, gazing with a non-focused look at the street from his 12th floor, crammed rented apartment at Prabhadevi, Jignesh was wondering how his life had come to this point. As he gazed out of his window into the busy hustle and bustle of people in the crowded street, he kept wondering every day what he was meant to be in this life and how he had ever landed there.

Every morning as he woke up, he barely had a vivid memory of what happened the previous night. As he looks at his short being in the mirror, he wonders. Sometimes he smirked, and sometimes he would be just about astonished. He started realising that every morning as he woke up, his hair was more than ruffled, his body was tired, as if he had done some physical exercise all night through. Lastly, he wondered why he had a glimmering band on his wrist, which, as far as he can remember, was never there when he dozed off. Contrary to that, he does distinctly remember that he did not wear any socks, but he always woke up wearing one. And they were indeed radiant, not to say colourful. Did he possess superpowers? What was this all about? He would ponder.

Days would pass, and every morning he was clueless, until one fine day he bought a video camera and placed it in his bedroom. The man had to find an answer. The next morning, he woke up tired but with a thought of mission accomplished and anxious as to what he was going to see. He zippily removed the memory card from the camera and connected it to his laptop. Two hours of footage, he discovered, as he clicked play! Thoughts crossing his mind like a rainbow in the dark.

Recording plays...

Jignesh opens the old trunk. A wave of anticipation rushes through his veins. He feels a surge of nostalgia as he pulls out the vintage tape recorder, its sleek curves and worn buttons reminding him of a bygone era. With a mix of excitement and haste, he grabs the cassette. Its faded label is barely visible, and he inserts it in the tape recorder with a satisfying click.

In a whirlwind of anticipation, Jignesh hastily slips into a golden, shimmering shirt that glitters under the soft light. He effortlessly slides into matching trousers, the fabric clinging to his body, ready to accentuate his every move. With a swift motion, he secures a goggle over his eyes, a stylish accessory that adds an air of mystery to his already captivating persona.

Eagerly, he retrieves a pair of white boots, their pristine shine reflecting the shimmering disco ball that hangs in his room. As he presses the play button on the tape recorder, a surge of energy pulses through the air. The room transforms into a kaleidoscope of pulsating lights and electrifying colours, immersing Jignesh in a dazzling spectacle.

The infectious beat of "I am a Disco Dancer" fills the room, instantly transporting Jignesh to a world of joy and freedom. With a mischievous grin, he begins to move, his body responding to the rhythm with an otherworldly fluidity. His limbs become a blur of motion as he effortlessly glides, spins, and grooves to the music, his energy growing with each passing second.

Time becomes a blur as Jignesh loses himself in the music, his dance becoming a mesmerising display of passion and skill. Two hours fly by in an instant, but for Jignesh, it feels like a lifetime of pure ecstasy. He danced with unbridled enthusiasm, unleashing his deepest desires and embracing his true self.

With sweat glistening on his brow and a heart filled with exhilaration, Jignesh comes to a breathless halt. He stands in the centre of the room, his chest heaving, and surveys the scene before him – a space that has been transformed into a sanctuary of disco magic.

Recording stops...

In this remarkable dance marathon, Jignesh had discovered more than just his love for disco; he had discovered his purpose, his reason to live. The dance floor became his canvas, and with each graceful movement, he painted a vivid portrait of his deepest desires and dreams.

Filled with a newfound sense of purpose, Jignesh knew deep down in his heart that his journey had just begun. With the echoes of "I am a Disco Dancer" still reverberating in his soul, he steps out into the world, ready to spread the joy and liberation of disco wherever he goes.

"Jignesh Dholakia, the embodiment of rhythm and groove, becomes the disco's nocturnal maestro, effortlessly dancing through the realms of dreams."

In the depths of his being, Jignesh discovers an electrifying purpose that ignites his very existence. The desire to dance and revolutionise the world of disco consumes him entirely. It becomes the core of his being, connecting the dots of his unique style and charismatic demeanour.

At the Mumbai Disco Retro Night party, as the evening casts a captivating spell in his mind, Jignesh adorns himself in attire that resonates with his soul. Amidst a sea of vibrant costumes at the party, he finds himself perfectly at ease. Throughout the night, Jignesh dances with unbridled passion, unrestricted by any inhibitions. He remains true to himself, never faltering or growing weary.

The DJ's voice reverberates through the air, proclaiming that this very moment marked the final melody of the night. A twinge of disappointment flickered across Jignesh's face as he turned, anticipation swirling within him, waiting for the last song to envelop the dance floor. And then, as if guided by fate's invisible hand, his eyes locked onto a petite yet radiant young woman. Her joyful spirit emanated through every graceful bounce and sway.

In an enchanting instant, Jignesh felt an irresistible pull, drawing him towards her like a magnet to iron. With an audacious burst of confidence, he approached her, their gazes interlocking in a shared understanding. As the music pulsed through their veins, they surrendered themselves to the rhythm, their bodies intertwining in a whirlwind of passion and unity. Together, they danced as if time stood still, their hearts beating in sync with the pulsating beats of the final song.

In that extraordinary moment on the dance floor, their souls harmonised, and the world around them faded into obscurity. It was as if the universe conspired to bring them together, uniting their spirits through the language of dance. Each step, each twirl, and each leap became an expression of their shared euphoria and unspoken connection. They moved as one, fuelling each other's energy, creating a magnetic force that transcended the boundaries of the dance floor.

As the last notes of the song echoed into the night, a bittersweet realisation washed over them. Their exhilarating dance had reached its conclusion, but their newfound bond lingered in the air. Walking hand in hand, their steps carried the echoes of their synchronised movements, and their vibrant colours merged seamlessly, a testament to their shared rhythm. In that moment, Jignesh knew he had discovered not only a dance partner but a kindred spirit—Alisha, the one who would dance beside him through the extraordinary journey of life.

Together, Jignesh and Alisha continued to dance, spreading their vibrant energy and love for disco wherever they went. They became a symbol of hope, reminding others to embrace their true selves, follow their passions, and find their own rhythm in this dance called life.

Chapter 14

Goldy

Prashant sat in his office on the 35th floor of a towering skyscraper, a testament to his rise in the corporate world. His office was a sleek, modern space with minimalist décor, where every piece of furniture seemed carefully chosen to reflect both professionalism and personal style. The walls were adorned with subtle yet striking artwork, while the large, floor-to-ceiling windows provided an uninterrupted view of the sprawling cityscape below.

Prashant, a man in his late thirties, was the embodiment of a successful corporate leader. His appearance was meticulously groomed. His hair was neatly trimmed, styled to perfection, and his face was clean-shaven, enhancing his sharp features. He wore a pair of stylish, designer glasses that not only aided his vision but also added an air of intellectual sophistication to his look. His attire was impeccable—a tailored suit in a dark, authoritative colour, paired with a crisp white shirt and a perfectly knotted tie. His polished shoes reflected the light from the tall window, hinting at his attention to detail.

As Prashant gazed out at the city, a mix of buildings, bustling streets, and green spaces spread out below him, he felt a sense of calm and determination. The city is alive with movement, from the tiny specks of cars navigating the streets to the distant outlines of people going about their daily lives. The horizon was dotted with other skyscrapers, each representing the ambitions and dreams of countless individuals. The sky, a blend of blues and pinks, with the setting sun casting a warm glow over the entire scene.

Despite the weight of responsibility on his shoulders, Prashant was at peace. He knew the challenges ahead were significant, but they were not insurmountable. His confidence was unwavering, a reflection of his journey from humble beginnings to the high-powered executive he is today.

Somewhere deep within, a voice echoes, "Yes, I can do it!" – a mantra that has carried him through many challenges and will continue to do so as he leads his team and his company to new heights.

Prashant, despite his current success, remains deeply and mentally connected to his humble beginnings in the bustling neighbourhood of Ghatkopar, Mumbai. He grew up in a chawl, a type of communal housing that is quintessentially Mumbai. The chawl where Prashant spent his childhood was a sprawling, old structure with narrow corridors that snaked through the building like a maze. The walls of the chawl were weathered, their original paint long faded and chipped, revealing layers of the building's history. Each floor was a hive of activity, with families living side by side in close quarters.

The 10ft x 10ft room that Prashant's family called home was tiny by any standard, but it was filled with love and hope. The room was sparsely furnished, with a small bed pushed against one wall and a wooden shelf that held their few possessions. A small stove in the corner served as the kitchen, and every inch of space was utilised efficiently. The single window in the room was their only connection to the outside world, offering a sliver of sky and a breath of fresh air in an otherwise cramped space. It was from this window that Savitri, Prashant's mother, would often look out, finding solace in the small patch of sky that reminded her of the wide-open spaces of her village.

The chawl itself was a microcosm of Mumbai's diverse population. People from various regions lived together, and the narrow corridors echoed with the sounds of different languages and dialects. The communal bathrooms and water taps were shared by all, leading to queues and chatter in the mornings and evenings. Women gathered at the entrance of the chawl, discussing daily matters, while children played cricket in the open space outside. The air was thick with the smell of cooking, the sounds of vendors calling out, and the occasional blare of a distant radio.

Savitri was a resilient woman, her spirit as strong as the iron grilles that covered the chawl's windows. Though she had only studied up to the 7th standard, she was wise beyond her years. Married young to Ramachandra, she left the comfort of her village to start a new life in Mumbai. The chawl's small room was a far cry from the spacious home she had known, but Savitri adapted quickly. She was practical and resourceful, managing the household with a sharp eye for every rupee. To support the family, she took on work as a housemaid in a nearby society. Her days were long, filled with cooking, cleaning, and taking care of her family, yet she never complained. For Savitri, every bit of sacrifice was worth it if it meant a better future for her son, Prashant.

Ramachandra, Prashant's father, on the other hand, was a man of few words but deep convictions. As an auto rickshaw driver, he spent long hours navigating the chaotic streets of Mumbai. His work was exhausting, but he took pride in it, knowing that his hard-earned money was going towards Prashant's education. Ramachandra was a man of principles, instilling in Prashant the values of honesty, hard work, and integrity. He believed that education was the key to a better life and made it his mission to ensure that Prashant received the best schooling they could afford. Though life in the chawl was tough, Ramachandra never wavered in his commitment to his family. His quiet strength and unwavering dedication were the bedrock to fulfil his dream of making Prashant an educated man.

As Prashant grew older, his parents, Savitri and Ramachandra, began to realise that their dreams for him seemed increasingly out of reach. By the time he was 7, it was clear that Prashant was not like the other children in the chawl. He was frail and lanky, his small frame accentuated by his bony arms and legs. His appetite was poor, and he often picked at his food, leaving most of it untouched. His weak physical condition made him look fragile, and he was easily overwhelmed by his emotions. Prashant was often teary-eyed, especially after school, where he would return home crying, complaining that the other children had teased him. They would call him names, mock his appearance, and taunt him for his timid nature.

The bustling life in the chawl was tough for a sensitive child like Prashant. The kids in the chawl were rough and competitive, especially when it came to cricket, the sport that dominated the tiny playground outside. Prashant was terrified of joining them, convinced that he would only become the target of more ridicule. He avoided the games, preferring to stay inside or find a quiet corner to play by himself. Even when his mother, Savitri, tried to intervene on his behalf, it was only a temporary solution. The teasing would stop for a day or two, but would resume soon after, and Prashant would retreat further into his shell.

Savitri, with her nurturing nature, was heartbroken to see her son struggle. She had always imagined Prashant growing up to be strong and confident, someone who could hold his own in the world. But as she watched him shy away from the other children, her heart filled with worry. On a few occasions, she confronted the other kids, scolding them for picking on Prashant. But deep down, she knew this wasn't a lasting solution. She realised that Prashant wasn't tough, and the world outside their small room would be even harsher.

Every night, after Prashant had fallen asleep, Savitri and Ramachandra would sit together in their dimly lit room, discussing their son's future. Their voices would be hushed, tinged with concern. Ramachandra, who had spent his life battling the city's chaos, knew all too well that the world was a tough place, especially for someone like Prashant. He believed in the survival of the fittest, and the thought of his son being too weak to navigate life's challenges kept him awake at night.

"We need to make him stronger," Ramachandra would say, his voice heavy with worry. "Life isn't easy, and he needs to learn to stand up for himself."

Savitri would nod in agreement, her heart aching as she thought about the difficulties her son would face. They both knew that something had to change. They couldn't protect Prashant from everything, but they could try to prepare him for the harsh realities of life. Every night, their discussions circled around this issue, trying to find a way to toughen Prashant up and help him build the resilience he would need to succeed in a world that wouldn't always be kind.

In these moments, Savitri and Ramachandra's love for their son was clear. Despite their limited means and the daily struggles of life in the chawl, their focus remained on Prashant's well-being. They were determined to give him the strength and confidence he needed to overcome his fears and face the world with courage.

"Thank you, Memsaab," Savitri whispered, her voice thick with emotion as Mrs. Shah handed her the crisp 2000 rupee note. It was Diwali, a time of celebration, and this unexpected bonus was more than just money to Savitri—it was a symbol of her hard work, a validation of her endless efforts. Tears welled up in her eyes, blurring her vision momentarily. She quickly blinked them away, but a few escaped, tracing a path down her weathered cheeks. With practiced ease, she rolled the notes and tucked them securely into her blouse, close to her heart. This small act held significance. This money would bring a rare moment of joy to her family, a joy that had been in short supply.

"Happy Diwali, Savitri!" Mrs. Shah called after her with a warm smile. But Savitri was already turning away, her mind racing with plans. She stepped out of the society's gate and into the bustling street beyond. The festive energy was palpable; the air was filled with the sound of firecrackers, the scent of freshly made sweets, and the sight of homes adorned with vibrant lights. Yet, Savitri moved with purpose, her eyes focused ahead, ignoring the festive distractions around her. She had a clear destination in mind, as if she were on a mission that had been predefined and rehearsed in her mind for days.

As she reached the corner where the street curved, she slowed down, her heart beating a little faster. 'Pental Pet Fish' store came into view, a small shop with large glass tanks lining its windows. The tanks were filled with water, each one a miniature world of colour and life. Inside them swam tiny, delicate fish of every hue—brilliant blues, radiant oranges, soft yellows. The gravel at the bottom of the tanks was a vibrant mix of colours, and small decorative plants swayed gently in the water, creating an enchanting underwater landscape.

The shop was modest, with its walls adorned with posters of various types of fish, but to Savitri, it was a place of magic. She had walked past it many times, always in a hurry to complete her chores, but each time, she had stolen a glance at the bright fish tanks. Today, however, was different. Today, she had come here with a purpose.

Savitri's hand instinctively reached for the money tucked inside her blouse. The feel of the crisp notes against her fingers gave her a surge of confidence. She stepped inside the shop, her eyes immediately drawn to a tank filled with tiny, iridescent fish that sparkled like jewels. She knew exactly which one she wanted. A small, simple tank with a few colourful fish that she had been eyeing for months. It was not just about the fish; it was about bringing a little bit of joy and beauty into their tiny 10ft x 10ft home. The fish tank would be something special for Prashant, a surprise that would light up his eyes, something to brighten their world amidst the daily struggles.

The shopkeeper greeted her with a friendly nod, recognising her from her previous visits. He had seen the longing in her eyes each time she stopped by, but today he noticed the determination in her step. "How can I help you?" he asked, sensing that this was the day she would finally make a purchase.

Savitri pointed to the tank she had already chosen in her mind. "I want that one," she said, her voice firm but soft, betraying the deep emotion behind this seemingly simple transaction.

As the shopkeeper prepared the tank, Savitri stood by, her heart swelling with a mix of anticipation and contentment. The sound of bubbling water and the sight of the tiny fish swimming gracefully filled her with a quiet joy. This purchase was not just about Diwali; it was a symbol of hope, a small reminder that beauty and happiness could exist even in the smallest of spaces.

Savitri carefully placed the fish tank on a small yet sturdy wooden table in the corner of their small 10ft x 10ft room. The soft glow of the tank's light illuminated the space, casting gentle reflections of water onto the walls. She knelt down beside it, her eyes wide with wonder as she observed the tiny world she had just brought into their home. Inside the tank, five little fish swam gracefully through the crystal-clear water, each one a vibrant splash of colour that brightened up their modest room.

As Savitri sat back and watched the fish settle into their new home, she felt a warmth spread through her chest. The tank was more than just a decoration; it was a symbol of hope, a tiny oasis of joy in their otherwise challenging life.

For now, though, the room was quiet, the only sound of the gentle hum of the tank's filter and the soft splash of water as the fish swam to and fro. Savitri felt a deep sense of satisfaction. The fish tank, with its vibrant, living jewels, had transformed their small, humble home into a place of magic and wonder. And in that moment, she knew that the 2000 rupees from Mrs. Shah had been well spent.

When Prashant came home from school that day, something immediately caught his eye. In the dimly lit corner of their small room, a soft, glowing light shimmered on a wooden table. He approached it slowly, his heart quickening with anticipation. As he got closer, he saw vibrant flashes of colour darting around inside a glass tank. It was a fish tank, filled with life, beauty, and a quiet magic that seemed to light up the entire room.

Prashant's eyes widened with wonder, his face breaking into a broad smile. It was as if an entirely new world had just been born before his very eyes, a world full of movement, colour, and possibility. Without a word, he turned to his mother and hugged her tightly, burying his face in her sari. His small arms clung to her, and in that embrace, Savitri felt the depth of his emotion. Tears welled up in her eyes as she stroked his hair. She had hoped the fish tank would make him happy, but she hadn't expected this—this overwhelming joy that now filled her son.

Every day, Prashant would rush home from school, eager to spend time with the fish. He'd sprinkle a little food into the tank, watching intently as the fish swam up to eat, their movements quick and precise. He had given each one a name, attaching a special meaning to each fish. The Betta fish, he called Lalu, for its bold red colour that reminded him of the vibrant sarees his mother wore on special occasions. The two Neon Tetras became

Nilu, named for their striking blue stripe that sparkled like the night sky.

But Prashant's favourite was the goldfish. He named him Goldy. This one in particular fascinated him. This goldfish was always full of energy, swimming around the tank as if he were the leader of the pack. Goldy had a certain spark in his movements, a confidence that seemed to ripple through the water, pushing the other fish to keep up with him. Prashant admired this about Goldy - the way he led with such ease, the way he seemed to embrace the whole tank as his own. Every day, Prashant's eyes would follow Goldy, studying him, learning from him.

As the days passed, something began to change in Prashant. The boy who was once frail and timid, who hardly ate and often cried from the teasing of other children, was now becoming someone new. He started to eat his meals without being coaxed, his appetite growing along with his spirit. His once lanky frame began to fill out, and there was a lightness to his step that hadn't been there before. He even started venturing outside to play cricket with the other kids in the chawl, something he had always been too afraid to do. The bouts of crying and complaining that had been a nightly routine in their household slowly faded away, until they disappeared almost entirely.

Savitri noticed the transformation in her son with a mix of surprise and relief. She often wondered what had brought about this change. What had given Prashant the strength to start facing the world with more confidence, to stand up to the challenges that once seemed insurmountable?

What Savitri didn't know was that Prashant's world had expanded far beyond their tiny room. The fish tank had become more than just a source of joy; it had become a source of inspiration. Every morning, as he sat watching the fish swim around, Prashant could almost hear Goldy speaking to him. "Yes, Prashant, you can do it!" the goldfish seemed to say, his movements bold and sure. The words echoed in Prashant's mind, filling him with a quiet determination. Whether he was at home, at school, or out playing, Goldy's voice was always there, pushing him forward, encouraging him to try harder, to be braver.

Day by day, those words, "Yes, you can do it" became a mantra that Prashant held close to his heart. They gave him the strength to face his fears, to overcome the teasing, and to grow into a stronger, more confident boy. He started to believe in himself in a way he never had before, and that belief began to shape his actions, his choices, his very outlook on life.

The fish lived for a couple of years, bringing constant joy to Prashant's life. But as all things must come to an end, so did the life of his beloved Goldy. Prashant felt a deep sadness, but something inside him had already changed irrevocably. Goldy may have been gone, but the words he had "spoken" lived on. "Yes, you can do it" had become more than just Goldy's words – they had become Prashant's own.

Years later, as Prashant sat in his high-rise office, overlooking the vast cityscape below, those words still echoed in his mind. Every morning when he woke up, every time he faced a challenge at work, he heard them. They were a reminder that he could face any obstacle, that he could achieve anything he set his mind to.

Goldy had never really spoken, of course. It was Prashant's mind that had transformed those quiet observations into a powerful internal voice. But that voice, that positive affirmation, had turned a timid, frail boy into a successful, confident man. And in the end, it wasn't just the fish that had changed Prashant – it was the belief that had taken root in his heart, the belief that we all need: the belief that we can do it.

Chapter 15

When Lightning Strikes

The blue *Bajaj Super* scooter roared down the highway, its engine straining as Amol twisted the throttle, pushing it to its limit. The wind whipped against their faces as they sped through the empty stretch of road, the tyres kicking up dust and debris in their wake. The sky above had grown ominously dark, the once clear horizon now swallowed by a mass of churning, angry clouds. Amol could feel the tension in the air, the humidity clinging to his skin, a sure sign that the heavens were about to unleash their fury.

Srirang, Amol's friend, clinging to the back of the stepney, could sense it too. His heart pounded in his chest; each beat a reminder of the precariousness of their situation. The scooter was flying at 65 kmph, the fastest it could go, but it didn't feel fast enough. The road ahead seemed endless, stretching out into the unknown, and with each passing second, the storm loomed closer, more threatening.

"Kadaaak!"

A deafening clap of thunder split the sky, reverberating through the air like the roar of an enraged beast. The sound was so intense that it felt as if the earth itself had trembled. In the next instant, the clouds above burst open, and the rain began to fall in sheets, hammering down with a force that seemed almost supernatural. It was as if the world had been plunged into chaos, the very elements conspiring against them.

Lightning cracked through the sky, jagged and blinding, illuminating the road ahead in eerie, fleeting flashes. Then, as if drawn by some malevolent force, one bolt of lightning struck the headlamp of the scooter. The light flickered violently, and for a split second, everything went white. Amol's vision blurred; his eyes were momentarily blinded by the searing brightness.

His hands tightened on the handlebars as he instinctively eased off the throttle, the scooter slowing down as if sensing the danger. The rain pounded against them, soaking through their clothes, making it hard to see and hard to breathe. The roar of the storm drowned out every other sound, leaving only the pounding of their hearts in their ears.

Amol's mind raced as he desperately searched for a safe place to stop. His thoughts were scattered, his senses overwhelmed by the intensity of the storm. The tree! He spotted a large tree just off the highway, its thick branches providing a small refuge from the deluge. He steered the scooter towards it, slowing to a crawl before finally coming to a halt beneath its sheltering canopy.

He killed the engine, the sudden silence almost as shocking as the storm itself. For a moment, they just sat there, the rain pouring down around them, the air thick with the smell of wet earth and ozone. Amol reached into his jacket pocket with trembling hands and pulled out a cigarette – Four Square Special. He lit it with shaky fingers, the small flame flickering in the gusts of wind, before taking a deep drag. The smoke filled his lungs, grounding him, giving him something to focus on besides the terrifying reality of what had just happened.

Srirang, still gripping to reality, looked at Amol with wide eyes. The fear was plain on his face, the realisation that they had just escaped something terrible by the narrowest of margins. He could hardly believe they were still alive, that the bolt of lightning hadn't sent them hurtling into the afterlife. The thought was almost too much to bear, the adrenaline still coursing through his veins, leaving him shaky and light-headed.

Amol exhaled slowly, the smoke billowing out in front of him. His mind was still reeling from the near-miss, his thoughts racing back to that blinding flash, the moment when time had seemed to stop. He knew that they had come terrifyingly close to something far worse than just a storm. It was as if death itself had reached out to them, only to withdraw at the last possible second, leaving them on the edge of oblivion.

As the rain continued to pour down, the two men sat in silence, their breaths heavy, their minds replaying the horror they had just survived. Amol took another deep drag from his cigarette, the burning ember glowing in the greyness, a small comfort against the chaos outside. He met Srirang's gaze, the unspoken understanding passing between them. They had missed a trip to hell by a fraction, and the reality of that was sinking in, heavy and undeniable.

Nature had crafted the perfect setting for a horror story, but somehow, they had managed to survive this chapter. The storm raged on around them, but under that tree, with the scooter parked and the cigarette burning down to its last, Amol and Srirang knew they had been given a second chance. And that knowledge, that brush with the brink, left a mark on them both, a reminder of how fragile life could be and how close they had come to losing it.

Amol, a 21-year-old student, was navigating his final year of B.Sc. Chemistry at Fergusson College in Pune. Though born and raised in the bustling city of Mumbai, he had moved to Pune to complete his graduation. The shift in pace was a welcome change for Amol; the hurried, chaotic rhythm of Mumbai life had given way to the laid-back, more relaxed atmosphere of Pune. Here, he relished his independence, living alone in a small, rented apartment, where he was free to set his own routine.

One of Amol's most cherished possessions was his father's old Bajaj Super scooter, a true vintage piece that had been manufactured in the 1970s. The scooter had been meticulously restored to its former glory, with every part shining as if it were brand new. Riding it gave Amol a sense of connection to his past, a tangible link to his father and his roots in Mumbai. Despite its age, the scooter ran smoothly, its engine purring like a well-cared-for machine. It was his trusted companion on the daily rides to college, as well as on the more spontaneous adventures that defined his life in Pune.

Amol's days were spent in a carefree blur of lectures & practical, hanging out with friends, and indulging in the little rebellions of youth. He had a tight-knit group of friends, but none were closer to him than Srirang, his classmate and confidant. The two of them were inseparable, often found together in the college canteen, bunking classes to catch the latest movies, or zipping through the streets on his scooter. Their friendship had grown thick over the past year, and they shared a bond that felt more like brotherhood.

One particular night in October, the two found themselves at their usual haunt – a dingy bar tucked away in a forgotten corner of the FC Road. The place wasn't much to look at, but it was perfect for them: cheap quarter of Old Monk rum, complimentary munching, no-questions-asked atmosphere, and a staff that had come to know them well. The waiters greeted them with nods of recognition, and the familiarity made the place feel like a second home.

On that night, after downing a quarter of Old Monk between them, a wild idea took root in their alcohol-fuelled minds. Amol, with his usual sense of adventure, suggested they take a midnight ride to Chiplun, a small town nearly 300 kilometres away, to visit his grandmother. The idea was ludicrous—300 kilometres on an old scooter, in the dead of night, and in their current state? It was the kind of harebrained scheme only the young and reckless would dream up.

But the thought of the journey thrilled them. The scooter, despite its age, seemed almost to shudder with anticipation as Amol mentioned the plan, as if it too was eager for the adventure. At 11:00 PM, they stumbled out of the bar, the cool night air hitting them like a splash of reality. But they were undeterred. They tanked up the scooter at the nearest fuel station, zipping up their jackets and strapping on their helmets, preparing themselves for the journey ahead.

As they mounted the scooter, the reality of what they were about to do finally began to sink in. The roads were empty, the streetlights casting long shadows that flickered as they rode past. The sky overhead was clear, the stars twinkling down as if to wish them luck on their madcap journey. The thrill of the unknown, of what lay ahead on that long, winding road, was electric. They weren't just riding to Chiplun – they were riding into the heart of an adventure, one that would test their resolve, their friendship, and the limits of their beloved Bajaj Super.

Amol revved the engine. The scooter roared to life, and they shot off into the night, the road stretching out before them like a promise. What lay ahead was uncertain, but in that moment, none of it mattered. They were young, they were free, and the world was theirs for the taking.

Amol and his friend Srirang had embarked on what was meant to be an exhilarating adventure – an overnight scooter ride from Pune to Chiplun. The route they had chosen wound through Wai and Mahabaleshwar before descending the treacherous Poladpur Ghat, promising a journey as thrilling as it was challenging. The plan was to reach Mahabaleshwar, rest until morning, and then complete the remaining distance to Chiplun.

The night air grew colder as they climbed the winding roads towards Mahabaleshwar. Mountain on one side and a dark valley on the other. The temperature dropped sharply, and the chill cut through their jackets, making every minute of the journey feel longer. By the time they arrived in Mahabaleshwar around 2:00 AM, they were shivering uncontrollably. Their spirits dampened by the biting cold. Exhausted and hungry, they searched for a place to rest, but their efforts were in vain. The town was either fully booked or asleep, and the guards at various lodges turned them down.

In their weary state, they stumbled upon an Anda Bhurji cart (egg cart) near the exit to Poladpur Ghat. The vendor, a south Indian Anna, a friendly middle-aged man with a welcoming smile, immediately noticed their predicament. He listened with curiosity as they explained their journey and offered them a quarter of Old Monk rum to warm them up. The gesture was more than just a simple kindness; it was a lifeline. Amol and Srirang gratefully accepted, downing the rum in quick succession. The warmth from the liquor seemed to revive them, chasing away the cold and fatigue.

As Amol and Srirang huddled close to the Anda Bhurji cart, Anna - a seasoned man with a hearty smile—got to work preparing their scrambled eggs. The cart was a modest setup, with a large iron griddle sizzling away over a small portable stove. The air was filled with the tantalising aroma of spices and cooked eggs, a comforting scent that promised warmth and sustenance.

Anna moved with practiced efficiency. He reached into a cooler under the cart and pulled out a handful of fresh eggs, their shells gleaming with a faint sheen. With a deft flick of his wrist, he cracked the eggs open, letting the yolks and whites spill into a metal bowl. The bowl was soon filled with a mixture of golden yolks and frothy whites.

He whisked the eggs vigorously, his movements producing a rhythmic clinking sound as the whisk hit the sides of the bowl. The eggs were then set aside, as he turned his attention to the griddle. A dollop of butter was scooped onto the hot surface. As it melted, it released a buttery fragrance that mingled with the spice-laden air.

Next, Anna added a finely chopped mix of onions, green chilies, and tomatoes to the sizzling ghee. He stirred the mixture with a metal spatula. The vibrant colours of the onions and tomatoes contrasted with the deep golden hue of the butter, creating a visual feast.

He added a generous sprinkle of spices: turmeric, cumin, coriander, and red chili powder. Each spice was carefully measured and added to enhance the flavour. The spices were roasted briefly to release their essential oils, filling the air with a rich, aromatic scent that made Amol and Srirang's stomachs growl in anticipation. The process was fast and rhythmic as the eggs began to set and form a fluffy texture. The dish was seasoned with salt.

As the Anda Bhurji cooked, it filled the air with a mouth-watering aroma. Anna skillfully scooped portions of the steaming, spicy scrambled eggs onto plates, each serving generously. He handed the plates to Amol and Srirang with a cheerful nod, wishing them a "Happy Journey".

Amol and Srirang eagerly dug into their meal. Each bite was a delightful combination of heat, spice and savoury goodness, the warmth of the dish seeping through their chilly bodies and reviving their spirits. The rich flavours and satisfying texture of the Anda Bhurji were a perfect antidote to the cold and fatigue they had been feeling.

With their hunger satiated and their spirits lifted, Amol and Srirang thanked Anna profusely. They paid him extra as a token of their gratitude, appreciating not only the meal but also the kindness and camaraderie that came with it. As they prepared to continue their journey, the warmth of the Anda Bhurji and Anna's good wishes lingered with them, giving them the energy and resolve to face the next leg of their adventure.

The descent from Mahabaleshwar to Poladpur Ghat was nothing short of a harrowing ordeal. The narrow road, barely wide enough to accommodate a single truck, wound precariously down the mountain, presenting a formidable challenge to Amol and Srirang. Each turn seemed to bring new dangers, as if the road itself were a living entity intent on testing their resolve.

The darkness enveloped them like a heavy shroud, broken only by the harsh beam of the scooter's headlamp. The light cut through the inky blackness, revealing a narrow, sinuous path that seemed to twist and turn endlessly. The cold, which had initially seemed like a mere inconvenience, now pierced through their jackets with a relentless bite, seeping into their bones and making each breath visible in the chilly night air.

Amol's knuckles were white as he gripped the handlebars, his focus absolute. The path ahead was a sheer drop on one side, the valley below a shadowy abyss that seemed to yawn wider with every bend. There were no guardrails or barriers to prevent a fall, only the stark emptiness of the cliffside. The sensation of danger was palpable; each curve of the road a potential precipice.

As they descended, the road itself seemed to come alive. Every twist was treacherous, demanding precise control and unwavering concentration. The scooter's tyres skidded slightly on loose gravel, sending a shiver of apprehension through Amol. He could feel the strain in his arms as he fought to keep the scooter steady, the engine's growl a constant reminder of the precariousness of their situation.

The darkness was almost suffocating, broken only by brief flashes of the headlamp illuminating jagged rocks and steep slopes. Each time the scooter's light flickered over a particularly sharp turn, Amol's heart skipped a beat, anticipating the possibility of a sudden drop or an unexpected obstacle. The cold, once again, became a fierce adversary, numbing his fingers and making the handlebars feel slick and slippery.

Srirang clung tightly to Amol, his breath coming in short, nervous bursts. The fear was evident in his eyes as he glanced over the edge, the vast chasm below a stark reminder of the consequences of any misstep. Despite his anxiety, he tried to stay calm, offering occasional words of encouragement to Amol, though they were barely audible over the roar of the engine and the wind.

The descent seemed to stretch on endlessly, each minute feeling like an eternity as they navigated the treacherous terrain. The road twisted and turned with a cruel indifference, as if daring them to falter. The pressure was unrelenting, every corner requiring a delicate balance of speed and control.

Finally, as the first light of dawn began to creep over the horizon, the descent gradually began to ease. The road levelled out, and the sheer drops gave way to more stable ground. Amol let out a sigh of relief, the tension in his body slowly unwinding as they emerged from the perilous ghat onto a flatter stretch of road. The scooter's engine roared with newfound vigour, as if acknowledging their successful navigation of the daunting descent.

Despite the challenges and the cold that still clung to them, a sense of triumph washed over Amol and Srirang. They had braved the treacherous descent, faced their fears and emerged victorious. The experience had tested their endurance and resilience, but it also brought them closer together, forging a bond of shared adventure and unwavering courage.

As dawn approached, they finally emerged from the ghat onto the flatter roads below. The sight of a small tea stall brought immense relief. They stopped to warm up, savouring the hot tea that soothed their chilled bones and revitalised their spirits. The sun was beginning to rise, casting a gentle light over the road as they pressed on, their excitement building with each kilometre closer to Chiplun.

By 8:00 AM, Amol and Srirang finally arrived at Amol's grandmother's home in Chiplun. The sun was just beginning to cast a warm glow over the landscape, and the air was filled with the sweet scent of blooming flowers from the garden surrounding the quaint home.

Amol's grandmother was a striking figure of elderly grace. Her silver hair was neatly tied in a bun, and her face was lined with the gentle creases of age and wisdom. She wore a traditional green saree with intricate gold embroidery that shimmered in the morning light. Her eyes, a warm brown, sparkled with a mixture of surprise and joy as she saw her grandson standing at her doorstep. The sight of Amol, whom she hadn't seen in nearly three years, brought an immediate, radiant smile to her face, a smile that seemed to light up the entire room.

The house itself was a charming reflection of simplicity and comfort. The exterior was painted in soft pastels, blending harmoniously with the surrounding greenery. A small, well-tended garden with colourful flowers and lush plants framed the entrance, adding a touch of vibrancy to the serene setting. The wooden door, adorned with a brass knocker, creaked open to reveal a cosy interior filled with the aroma of home-cooked meals.

Inside, the house was a haven of warmth and hospitality. The walls were lined with family photographs and mementos, capturing moments of joy and togetherness over the years. The living room, with its wooden furniture and handwoven rugs, exuded a homely charm. A large brass thali, with an array of fruits and traditional sweets, was set out on the coffee table, a welcome gesture for the weary travellers.

As Amol and Srirang stepped inside, the home seemed to envelop them in a comforting embrace. The grandmother's joyful laughter rang through the rooms as she enveloped Amol in a tight, affectionate hug. Her hands, though aged and slightly trembling, held him with a firmness that conveyed her deep love and relief.

The reunion was filled with heartfelt conversations and shared memories. Amol's grandmother regaled them with stories of Amol's father as a child—tales of his mischievous adventures, his achievements, and the simple joys of growing up in Chiplun. Each story was accompanied by expressive gestures and laughter, bringing the past to life in vivid detail.

The meals prepared were a feast of local flavours. Fresh mangoes, their golden flesh bursting with sweetness, were served alongside roasted cashew nuts that were both crunchy and savoury. The kitchen was a bustling hub of activity, with Amol's grandmother preparing traditional dishes that had been passed down through generations. The aroma of spicy fish curries, hot rice, and freshly made chapatis filled the air, creating an irresistible invitation to savour the comfort of home-cooked food.

Over the next two days, Amol and Srirang immersed themselves in the warmth of their grandmother's love.

They spent their mornings chatting with the grandmother on the veranda, enjoying the cool breeze and the view of the distant hills. Afternoons were filled with strolls through the garden, where Amol reminisced about his childhood visits and the changes that time had brought. Evenings were spent around the dining table, sharing stories, laughter, and the delectable dishes that Amol's grandmother prepared with loving care.

The time spent at his grandmother's home was a balm for Amol's soul, offering a respite from the rigours of their journey and a chance to reconnect with his roots. The affection and hospitality extended by his grandmother created a cocoon of comfort and belonging, making the visit an unforgettable chapter in his life. As they prepared to leave, the farewell was bittersweet, marked by promises to return and the lingering warmth of family ties that had been rekindled during their stay.

When it was time to return, the journey took on a new intensity. As they set out around 10:00 AM, the weather took a turn. Dark clouds rolled in, and the sky opened up with a torrential downpour. The ride back was fraught with the same uncertainty and danger they had faced on the way to Chiplun, but this time, the rain made the roads slick and hazardous. The lightning had struck the headlight of the scooter, narrowly missing them.

As Amol took a deep drag from his cigarette during a brief rest stop, he reflected on the journey. The experiences of the past few days had underscored a profound realisation: life is unpredictably fragile. The dangerous twists of the Poladpur Ghat, the sudden downpour on the return trip, and deadly lightning had brought into sharp focus how quickly circumstances can change. What had started as a thrilling adventure had also become a reminder of life's inherent uncertainties.

The journey was more than just a trip to visit family; it was a testament to the unpredictability of life and the resilience required to navigate it. The risks they faced, the unexpected kindness of a stranger, and the sheer unpredictability of their adventure served as a poignant reminder that while life may be full of unforeseen challenges, it is also filled with moments of unexpected joy and connection. The moral of their journey was clear: embrace the adventure, be prepared for the unpredictable, and treasure the moments of clarity and connection along the way.